# INFLUENCERS JUST WANNA HAVE FUN

## TIME TRAVELERS #3

TERESA YEA

Visit me at teresayea.com
Sign up for my newsletter

ALSO BY TERESA YEA


Time Travelers (Chick Lit)

An Influencer in King Arthur's Court (#1)

Regency Influencer (#2)

Influencers Just Wanna Have Fun (#3)


Indigo Bay Series (Romantic Comedy)

Pixely Ever After (#1)

Once Upon a Photo Booth (#2)

Symphony in the Snow (#3)

Tea for Two (#4)


Bookish Romantics (Romantic Comedy)

Awkward in October (#1)

The Plant Nanny (#2)


Golden Age of Monsters (Dark Fantasy Romance)

Love in a Time of Monsters (#1)

Empire of Sand (prequel)


Gothic Horror

Black Heart, Red Ruby (standalone)

I sock Merlin in the arm. *"What. Did. You. Do?"*

I'm enraged, which is putting it mildly.

Merlin (my hot wizard companion), Vicky (my bitchy lawyer cousin), and me (your friendly neighborhood influencer) are strapped into the jungle boat of Jurassic Park: The Ride.

We'd just plummeted eighty-five feet into what would normally be a big *SPLASH*...

Except there was no splash.

Or a water tank.

Or ride attendants.

We're in a giant dirt field, surrounded by sagebrush and weeds. The water tank could have cushioned our fall. Now I have whiplash and my body aches like a battered birthday piñata.

We're still at Universal Studios Hollywood — a bare bones version of the theme park. Where's the big crowds? The food vendors? The Wizarding World of Harry Potter? There's only a dated version of the tram tour and a thin line of guests, all of them dressed like they walked right out of the '80's:

Pastels and perms.

Oversized T-shirts and spandex tights.

Side ponytails and neon friendship bracelets.

Acid wash jeans and scrunched up gym socks.

Any normal person would think we dropped in on '80s Day at Universal Studios.

I am not a normal person.

I have seen some shit.

My name is Laurel Kirby. I used to be an influencer with 125k followers until I met Morgaine le Fey, an evil sorceress with epic cheekbones and mad hacker skills. She installed MorgVPN on my phone and sent me back to Camelot, where I had a brief stint as the royal influencer to King Arthur. At court I taught Merlin, Arthur's sexy advisor, to read the internet. He's been my time-traveling companion (re: thorn in my side) ever since.

I whack Merlin across his rock hard stomach. "Don't tell me you reprogramed MorgVPN!"

Merlin's sexy sinister face is the picture of bewilderment. "I did not touch MorgVPN." He pushes on the safety bar of our boat and hops onto the dirt. He offers me a hand.

I clamber out after him. "Well, if you didn't, who did?"

Merlin twists his neck from side to side. *Pop* goes his muscles. He groans in relief. "I do not know."

I check the seats behind me. "What happened to the other people in the boat?" We were packed in with at least seven other riders who have all mysteriously vanished. Hopefully they were not turned into time dust.

"What's the date?" Vicky groans beside me. Her attention is pinned on a kid holding a Rainbow Brite doll.

I yank out my iPhone and check the lock screen. "November 13."

*"The year!"*

"Allow me to answer that," says a familiar husky voice.

A woman with blade-like cheekbones stands before us, her mile-long legs planted apart in a warrior-stance. Her raven-black hair has been permed and teased like Hairstyle #3 in those dated beauty salon posters. She's wearing a slinky gold cocktail dress with a giant bow at the waist and enormous shoulder pads, black nylon stockings, and matching gold pumps. Her eyes are ringed in heavy purple eyeshadow and her cheekbones, already her most prominent feature, are slashed with lavender blush. I know contouring is all the rage, but Morgaine le Fey is taking it to the next level.

"Ever heard of blending with a beauty sponge?" I ask, unable to take my eyes off her cheekbones.

Morgaine props a hand on her trim waist. "Laurel Kirby..." she says with a shake of her permed head. "Still concerned with trivial matters while the world burns around you."

I sniff. "I hardly think a bad make-up job is trivial."

Morgaine's gaze passes over me and lands on Merlin. "Nice shorts."

Merlin is wearing a pair of shorts from Zara Men (shout-out to Zara Men!) because he kept complaining about the hot Los Angeles weather. And okay, his legs, while shapely from years of horseback riding, are on the pasty side. It's not like he can help it. He's lived in the Dark Ages all his life.

Merlin yanks off his sunglasses. "Le Fey, you bloody witch! What manner of vile magic have you inflicted upon us now?"

Morgaine shoots him a patronizing smile and shifts her attention to my cousin.

Vicky stands up and glares at Morgaine. Not long ago (and by that I mean yesterday), Morgaine kidnapped Vicky during her wedding and spirited her away to Regency England, where they became lovers until Morgaine shrank her into the size of an action figure. It's a long story... suffice to say, Morgaine just earned a top slot on Vicky's shit list.

Morgaine gives Vicky a scant nod of acknowledgment. "Victoria."

Vicky shakes the dust out of her sleek corporate bob. "Bitch."

Morgaine shrugs. "Nice to see you too."

"Cut the crap, Morgaine," I step in. "Where the hell *are* we?"

Morgaine crosses her arms, flexing her powerful shoulders pads. A stray breeze blows back her fluffy perm. "You're in 1987."

1987?!

"This is bullshit!" Vicky says.

Merlin slaps his forehead. "The future! We're in the future!"

"Stop it," I lower my voice. "You're embarrassing me. 1987 is not the future."

"It is to me," he says.

What can you expect from a time traveling companion from the Dark Ages? He's excited by indoor plumbing and surprised that we've banned torture by hot oil.

"1987? This really sucks." I rake my fingers through my hair, letting the date sink in. I was just a twinkle in my parents' eyes. "Why? Why in the world would you send us here?"

Morgaine comes forward with beseeching eyes. "I need your help."

I poke myself in the chest. "Me?"

"You."

"Seriously?"

"Totally."

I snort. "I bet you do."

"I do." Morgaine nods. She sounds sincere enough.

Here we go again...

Morgaine's been obsessed with me ever since I walked into her gift shop and tried her ridiculously easy challenge of yanking a *fake* sword from a *fake* stone. All I wanted was my picture on the winner's wall. I got more than I bargained for. Morgaine somehow got it in her thick skull that I'm the rightful Queen of England and has been stalking me ever since.

I was dumb enough to get sucked into her royal takeover plan in Regency England. We ended up kidnapping and *shrinking* the King, Prince regent, and a handful of Parliament members and stuffing them in my purse. Boppin' men on the head and shrinking them to the size of toy soldiers is both weird and mean. It's an experience I'd rather not repeat.

"You're set on another royal takeover, aren't you? Because if you brought me back here to take out Princess Di and marry Prince Charles, I'm not doing it. He's not my type and you're going to have to kill me before I wear that wedding dress!"

"I didn't send you here to take over the British throne," Morgaine says, "though if you felt *inclined* that would be a bonus..."

I exchange a three-way eye roll with Vicky and Merlin. "Nope."

Morgaine shrugs. Can't knock an evil sorceress for trying. "I brought you back to 1987 because I need help with Mordred."

"Mordred?" I meet Merlin's gaze. The mention of Morgaine's secret baby with her brother Arthur is a sore spot for Merlin. The king's incest baby was pretty bad for royal PR, and I'm not 100% convinced Merlin isn't still planning to — *you know* — get rid of Mordred.

I know. *I know.* Baby murder sounds horrifying to our modern sensibilities. It's totally a thing in Merlin's world where everyone and their mother indulges in a little bloodshed just to stay alive.

Merlin has never mentioned his past, so I did a little internet sleuthing. I'm not completely dense. I can Wikipedia with the best of them. Someone tried to murder Merlin in the crib *and* he thwarted an assassination attempt on infant Arthur Pendragon. Baby murder... a toxic cycle amongst the royals.

"Who's Mordred?" Vicky asks.

Yikes! I forgot that Vicky was not a part of our Medieval adventures.

"My son," Morgaine says.

Vicky's eyes widen. *"You have a son?"*

Uh oh. Guess Morgaine failed to mention her baby baggage when she was seducing my cousin. "You'll never guess who's the father," I add. I can't help myself. I like gossip. It's a sickness.

Vicky glares at Morgaine. "Who?" She whirls on Merlin. "Him?"

Merlin scowls. "Ha! I would rather have my eyes gouged out by a rusty nail than bed that witch."

Morgaine rolls her eyes. "You flatter yourself to think I would ever bed an old goat like you."

"Nay," Merlin says, slipping back to his native tongue (English with a touch of Shakespeare). "You would rather bed your own brother."

*Sic burn.*

Vicky gasps. "You slept with your brother?!"

"*Half* brother. We were at a festival!" Morgaine sighs.

"I was at Coachella," Vicky says. "But *I* didn't sleep with my brother."

"No offense," I point out, "your brother isn't hot."

"I wouldn't sleep with Leon even if he *was* hot because he's my brother."

I turn to Morgaine. "What's the matter with Mordred? Is he colic? Diaper rash?" I have fond memories of Baby Mordred. He was so cute and he smelled good for a Medieval baby (most of them stunk to high heaven). I can't wait to kiss his chubby cheeks and pinch his bread roll arms. "Where is he? Can I hold him?"

"He's in Miami."

"Miami! What's he doing there? I hope you left him with a reputable nanny."

A dark squall passes over Morgaine's face. "He's not a baby anymore."

"Right. Why did I think Mordred's still a baby? He must be pushing fifteen hundred years old."

"Fourteen hundred and eighty-eight, to be exact," Morgaine says.

"They grow up so fast."

Morgaine and I share a bittersweet sigh.

"Is he well?" I ask. "Why is he living in Miami?"

"Because he's a dumbass." She clears her throat. "Mordred got mixed up with a bad crowd."

"Like a gang?"

Morgaine nods. "Something like that. He's..." She lowers her head and bites her bottom lip.

"Morgaine?" I step forward. "Are you...?" Omigod. She is! I see tears. Real *human* tears. Her make-up is a mess.

"He's mixed up in drugs," she says.

I gasp. "Mordred? Drugs? Like pot? Heroin? Coke?"

Merlin whispers, "I have sampled Coke. It is good."

"Not that kind of coke," Vicky says.

"Mostly cocaine," Morgaine says. "He's snorting it like it's going out of style."

"Ew." I'm shook. "Baby Mordred's junkie?"

"No! Yes!" Morgaine chokes back a sob and seizes me by the shoulder. "That's why I brought you back, Laurel. I need you to come with me to Miami. He's out of control! He won't listen to me, but he'll listen to you."

"Me?" I frown. "Why me?"

"You were his favorite."

"He remembers me? He was three months old."

"You two had a special bond," Morgaine says. "And he always stopped crying when you held him."

I stand a little taller. Babies love me. I give off comforting vibes.

"What about Merlin?" I check over my shoulder and take a gander at Merlin's brooding face. "He bounced Mordred on his knee once."

"Him... not so much," she says. "But he can come too. I need all the muscle I can get."

That sounds ominous. Is she expecting to find Mordred in a cocaine rage?

"And Vicky? She's coming too, right?"

Morgaine eyes her former lover. "Believe me, Mordred will need a lawyer after this."

"I'm a divorce attorney," Vicky says.

"Close enough."

Vicky folds her arms across her chest. "Then you're getting a bill."

"Will you do it?" Morgaine presses me. "Will you help Mordred?"

"I don't know... Last time we worked together you called me a numbskull and had your pterodactyl attack me, amongst other things..."

Morgaine holds up her palms, calling for a truce. She's sporting blood red acrylic nails. With a flick of her wrist, I'm sure she could scratch my eyes out. I keep my distance.

"I solemnly swear I will do no harm in 1987," she says. "Please..." her eyes searches mine. "It's my *son* we're talking about."

"I don't know what to say to Mordred. I barely know him."

"You're an influencer. Influence him! Tell him to just..." She furls her hands into fists as she searches for the right words to convince me to join her rehab campaign. "Just say 'no' to drugs."

## 3

---

JUST WHEN I thought I was out, Morgaine pulls me back in.

After she chased me around London on her pterodactyl, I swore I would never team up with her again. Yet here I am: part of Morgaine's entourage. It's like an abusive relationship. Morgaine *literally* knocks me around and then woos me back with empty promises. Except this time it's different. Morgaine is not after world domination. She's just a mother worried about her son.

*I'm doing this for Baby Mordred.*

What's the point of being an influencer if I can't use my powers of persuasion for a good cause? Besides, I have bigger things to worry about than Morgaine betraying me again.

We're huffing through the theme park to keep up with Morgaine's power walk as she leads us to the parking lot.

I keep my eyes pointed straight ahead. No big movements. I like attention. The good kind of attention. Right now I feel like the dorky new kid walking down the hall to math class. Avoid eye contact. No sudden movements unless I attract the notice of a bully who's itching to give me a wedgie. By the way, do bullies give wedgies anymore? Is that a thing? Okay. It's been a long time since I've been in high school and my memories are heavily influenced by *Back to the Future* and *Saved by the Bell.*

"Is it me? Or is everyone staring at us?"

Merlin and Vicky glance around. Merlin scowls at a group of gawking middle schoolers. The leader, a kid with preppy Ken Doll hair, points at us and his minions laugh.

Vicky edges closer to the pack. "Why are people staring at us?"

My influencer senses are on high alert. I'm having major flashbacks...

Sophomore year of high school. I'm wearing last season's neon pink skinny jeans while everyone was dressed in neutral colors. We're talking blue, black, and military-green denim. I stood out like a sore thumb. And while no one said anything to my face, my 'friends' mocked me behind my back and bullied me on Twitter.

I'd made a major fashion faux pas and it's haunted me for years. *Years!*

Between you and me, I still get nightmares about it. Like I'll wake up in a cold sweat and immediately have to take an intensive inventory of my closet, making sure every item is still in style.

This trauma is the reason why I thrived as an influencer. I'm attuned to trends, terrified of being out of style. You'll never catch me rocking slouchy riding boots over tights like it's 2010.

As more people silently judge our outfits, I glance down at my clothes.

I'm in a plain white crop top and cut off denim shorts.

Vicky is in a black T-shirt, jeans, Birkenstocks.

And Merlin is in a comfortable yet monochromatic blue-grey outfit.

It's not like we coordinated our theme-park outfits, but we just naturally gravitate toward a minimalist color palette. Less is more. We're on trend... in our time.

I take a closer look at everyone around us.

Lace.

Pastels.

Neon.

Leather.

Chains.

Leg warmers.

Big hair.

Heavy make-up.

I check out Morgaine's perm, glitzy cocktail dress, and heels. She fits right in whereas the three of us stick out like a sore thumb.

"Oh my God..." I cross my arms in a self-conscious attempt to hide my outfit. "Don't you see what's going on here?"

"What?" Merlin stiffens and follows my horrified gaze.

"We're out of style for 1987!" I eye a woman in a pink tutu and leather jacket. She has one studded motorcycle glove, not two. "We're too boring!"

Merlin looks down at his monochromatic outfit. "They must think we're serfs!"

My stomach bottoms out. "Worse. Like we don't belong in the Valley."

"What Valley?" Merlin asks.

"The San Fernando Valley."

Morgaine turns over her shoulder, her lips hitched in that smug smirk I know and *despise*. "Chances are they think you're from an undesirable zip code. Below Sunset."

Vicky and I exchange a horrified look.

"I live in Brentwood!" Vicky says.

Morgaine shakes her head. "You don't look Brentwood," she says. "The three of you look like you shop at Goodwill."

I clasp a hand over my mouth. I feel faint. "Morgaine... I know Baby Mordred needs us, but..." I gesture to our bland-ass serf clothes. "We can't go to Miami like this."

Morgaine nods. "Frankly, I'm ashamed to be seen with you lot."

"This is fashion emergency," I say.

"I agree."

At last, we agree on something.

"Come," Morgaine says, leading us to her cheery red Ferrari Testarossa. "To the mall!"

4

"Look!" I tap Vicky on the shoulder. "A Sam Goody!"

"Where?"

"By the Radio Shack."

"This brings me back," Vicky says. "*Waay* back. Look! A Waldenbooks."

I shake my head in amazement. "They have everything at this mall."

Our eyes are wide as we pass the fountain. The Glendale Galleria is packed: teens in head to toe pastels, moms pushing strollers, couples holding hands. I can't remember the mall being this busy. Then again, I haven't been to the mall in years and on the rare occasion that I dropped by to pick up a last minute Christmas gift, the mall is dead, bleak, sad...

In 1987, the mall is alive and thriving.

We travel as a pack up the escalator and follow Morgaine to the food court where she treats us to an Orange Julius.

"Vicky!" I nearly choke on my drink. "I see your mom!"

She pokes her head up. "Where?"

"Outside KB Toys."

"Oh shit! She's with *your* mom!"

"*What?*"

"Omigod! My mom is wearing Morgaine's dress."

We both turn to Morgaine, who is standing in line at Hot Dog on a Stick and impatiently tapping her gold pumps on the coral tiles. Merlin has demanded a corn dog in addition to his Orange Julius and he's pretty persistent (see whiny) when he doesn't get his way.

"Do you think we should say hello?" I ask.

"No! It might freak them out."

"But they won't know who we are. We're not even born yet."

"Speak for yourself." Vicky cocks her head to the pudgy toddler at the end of a leash. "That's me."

My eyes widen. "No way! You were a leash kid?"

"Unfortunately."

Toddler Vicky is dressed in corduroy overalls with a teddy bear on the front and pink n' purple Velcro sneakers. Warmth floods me. "Oooh, Vicky! Look at those fat cheeks." I stand up. "Let's go say hello."

"Laurel! Get back here!"

Our moms enter the food court, gossiping in rapid fire Korean. I kneel down in front of chubby toddler Vicky. "Aren't you the cutest thing!" I greet Auntie June, who's rocking a puffy '80s perm. "Your daughter is totally adorable. Can I hold her?"

"Thank you," Auntie June says. "But no. Vicky doesn't like strangers."

"I bet she'll like me. I'm great with kids."

"She bites."

"That sounds like Vicky..."

"What?" Auntie June asks.

I clear my throat. "Icky. That sounds icky."

Auntie June and my mom size up my bland-as-hell outfit. Blood rushes to my cheeks. I can only imagine what they must be thinking. *Where'd you get that tank top? Kmart?*

My mom whispers in my aunt's ear, then squints at my face. "Do I know you?"

Good question. She *will* know me. I'm her favorite person in the world.

"Nope."

Vicky joins us and stares down at her toddler self. Mom and Auntie June size her up too, unimpressed by her sleek bob and minimalist outfit.

They check out her Birkenstocks and shake their heads. "Hippie," I hear my mom mutter.

"This is my cousin," I say. "Her name is Vicky too."

Little Vicky gnaws on the plastic hands of her Rainbow Brite doll. Spittle dribbles down her chubby chin. Big Vicky is having a surreal moment. It isn't every day you come face to face with your younger self.

If I had the opportunity to meet young Laurel, I'd advise myself to start my current skin care routine at thirteen, apply sunscreen even on cloudy days, and *moisturize, moisturize, moisturize...*

But Vicky being Vicky, she pries the Rainbow Brite doll from Toddler Vicky's mouth and peers very hard into Little Vicky's eyes. "Buy Apple stock."

"Goo!" Toddler Vicky says.

Vicky stands up and jots down something on a piece of scrap paper, which she presses into her startled mom's hands. "Remember these three companies. Apple. Tesla. Amazon. Buy tons of stock under Vicky's name," she says, "and whatever you do, don't let her go to law school."

Her mother slowly backs away. "Who is this crazy woman?" she asks my mom in Korean. "What does she want?"

"They are dressed like homeless people," my mom says. "Maybe they want money... Give them a dollar."

"I have a Sears gift card." Auntie June hands me her gift card. "That has ten dollars left," she says, "Buy clothes?"

I shake my head. "No. No."

"Yes. Yes," my mom presses.

Out of the corner of my eye, I spy Morgaine huffing toward us. Merlin trails behind her with two corn dogs and an extra large cup of lemonade.

"There you are!" Morgaine snaps. "How about giving me a heads up before you wander off to the toy store?"

"Who is she?" my mom asks.

Vicky and I stifle a giggle. "Our mother," we say, earning a nasty glare from Morgaine.

## 5

---

ACID WASH JEANS. Mint green blouse. Yellow scrunchy socks and spanking new Reeboks. I check myself out in the mirror.

"You know what?" I fluff up my crunchy new perm. "'80s fashion is growing on me." My jeans are pleated at the waist, tapered at the legs. "These are so comfortable."

"Get them," Morgaine says.

"What about these?" I hold up a canary yellow tennis skirt and matching polo shirt.

"Get them, too."

"Seriously?"

"Seriously."

I hold up a fistful of headbands. "What about these? I can't decide between lavender or this geometric pattern."

"Get them both." Morgaine scrutinizes her new manicure.

"No way."

"Way." She grins. "Anything your heart desires."

"Anything? Even the off-the-shoulder pink number at Robinson's May?"

"Go crazy."

I resist the urge to fist pump the air. First a makeover and now a shopping spree. "Never thought I'd say this: you're like, my favorite person right now."

I totally want to hug her. Given our history and the *many* times Morgaine has tried to kill me, a hug might be a little weird.

Morgaine is my sugar mama. I'm ready to forgive all the bad blood between us so long as she keeps buying me stuff. What can I say? I'm a material girl living in a material world.

I like '80s Morgaine better than all the versions of Morgaine I've met.

"How did you get to be so rich?" I ask.

"Generational wealth."

Makes sense. Morgaine's been around for ages.

"And I dated a Wall Street stockbroker," she adds, "but that relationship quickly went south."

"What happened?"

"Caught him snorting coke off another woman's ass."

I shift my eyes away. "That ought to do it."

Morgaine shrugs. "You win some, you lose some. He gave me his Ferrari as a parting gift."

Vicky swipes the dressing room curtain aside. "What do you think?" She picks at her massive shoulder pads. She's wearing an oversized electric blue blazer over a leather mini skirt, black tights, and white ankle boots. Yellow plastic hoops dangle from her ears. "Too much?"

"Get it," I say. "It's hot."

Morgaine checks out Vicky's mile long legs. The longing on her face doesn't escape my notice. Morgaine has it bad for my cousin. Guess she should have thought of that *before* she shrunk Vicky because there's no way in hell Vicky is ever going to forgive her.

"Wear the mini skirt to dinner," Morgaine says.

Vicky arches an eyebrow. "Where's dinner?"

"At the Sherman Oaks country club."

"Country club!" I share an excited glance with Vicky. "We've never been to the country club. Our parents were more Sizzler folks."

"Hey," Morgaine says. "It's the '80s. Live it up."

Merlin joins us from the men's department. Vicky and I freeze at the sight of his oversized linen suit, turquoise shirt, and loafers (no socks).

"Oh. My. God." I check out his naked ankles. His jacket is rolled up to the elbows, exposing his swanky gold Rolex. "You look like you stepped right out of Miami Vice."

"We *are* going to Miami, are we not?" Merlin's brows furrow as he tinkers with his new toy.

"Is that a Rubik's Cube?" I ask.

Merlin grunts in frustration. "I got it at the toy shop and it's bloody impossible! I've been at it for an hour."

I hold out my hand. "Give it here."

"*Really* Laurel?" Vicky shakes her head. "Merlin's a wizard."

I tip my chin up at a haughty angle. "What's that supposed to mean?"

"You're not exactly the brightest tool in the shed."

*Well!*

I arch an eyebrow. "Give me a moment." I work the cube with nimble fingers, twisting this way and that until each side is an uniformed color. I finish under three seconds flat. Take *that* Vicky. "Done."

Merlin takes the cube and scratches his head. "Amazing!"

Morgaine is more shook than when I pulled Excalibur from the stone at her gift shop.

But Vicky, having never witnessed my talents, gawks at me as if I'd just sprouted wings and a tail.

"How did you do that?" Vicky asks.

I flip my hair. "Like it's hard."

"This is why I need her to be my influencer," Morgaine says. "She has a specialized set of skills."

Vicky eyes me up and down. "What skills?"

"To this day," Morgaine taps her chin, "I still don't know what they are. I find it easier just to go with it."

6

We valet Morgaine's Ferrari Testarossa and slow-mo travel as a pack inside the country club. Heads turn at our arrival, sizing up our poofy dresses and even poofier hairdos.

Vicky sticks close to my side. "Why is everyone staring at us? Is it because we reek of Aqua Net?"

"It's because we're hot." I wink at the human Ken doll to my left. "What's 'hot' in '80s speak? Tubular? We're totally tubular."

Vicky shakes her head. "Stop, Laurel. Just stop." She eyes the aquamarine n' coral dining room, the servers carrying trays of shrimp cocktails, cheese balls, and brandy snaps.

"Look at the club members," Vicky whispers.

"I see them."

Lots of popped collars and tennis dresses.

"It's pretty WASP-y in here," she says, nodding to the silver fox in the navy blazer and khaki trousers. "And white."

"It's pretty white in here."

"'Pretty' white? *Very* white."

Okay. You should know by now that my cousin Vicky is terrified around white people. There. I said it. She's afraid of being colonized.

All her friends are Asian. Her law firm is deeply entrenched in the L.A. Asian community.

As her hapa cousin, I'm the whitest friend she has and we're not even friends. You should *see* how skittish she was in 1813 England, which is why her brief fling with Morgaine came out of nowhere. I, for one, was shook. Not because Vicky was engaged to a man and had an affair with a woman, but a pasty British sorceress? Very unlike Vicky. She would never pick vanilla ice cream over matcha green tea.

Morgaine must be great in bed.

"Morgaine!" Vicky says. "We're surrounded by Republicans."

"Yes, I suppose we are," Morgaine says.

"Are *you* a Republican?" I ask.

Morgaine shrugs. "Does it matter?"

"I bet she is," I murmur to Vicky.

"Wouldn't put it past her. She hates paying taxes."

*"Really?"*

Vicky lowers her voice. "Total tax evader."

"I knew it!"

Morgaine leads us to the fringes of an Olympic size swimming pool. An orange dusk settles on the suburbs. The air is cool, dry, and fragrant with expensive perfume. From our patio table, we can see a purple haze settle over the Simi Hills.

It's a peaceful night in the Valley.

*Too* peaceful.

So far, our '80s trip has been tame. Short of a jarring plummet into a dirt field, we hadn't been chased or attacked. Where's the serf mob? The Regency gentlemen out for blood? Where's the dinosaur abduction?

Merlin notices me squirm in my wicker chair. "What's wrong?"

I lean in and whisper in his ear. "I'm anticipating disaster. The '80s are too tame."

"Are you searching for danger?"

"Danger finds me."

A server comes to take our order.

I peer at the menu. Apricot chicken. Surf n' Turf. No prices. That's when you know the food is expensive. New York strip steak. Chicken a la King. Sushi? I glance around at the WASP-y diners. Somehow I can't see them snacking on sashimi.

"Get whatever you want," Morgaine says.

I eye Merlin and a silent message passes between us. *Why is she being so nice? There's got to be something up her sleeves.*

"Sushi?" Vicky says in surprise.

"Is that what you'll have?" The server asks.

"What kind of sushi is it?"

"The kind in the roll."

"What kind of fish?" Vicky presses because she's the kind of girl who badgers waiters with a million questions.

The server scratches his temple with his pencil. "I can check with the chef."

"See that you do — "

"She'll have the sushi," Morgaine snatches up Vicky's menu and hands it to the server.

Talk about domineering!

Vicky is shooting death lasers at Morgaine. I don't know what's going on between the two of them ... and I don't want to know.

The server clears his throat. Seems like he has the same idea. He turns to me with a tight smile. "And you, Miss?"

"Apricot chicken." What can I say? I'm vanilla.

"I am intrigued by this 'Surf n' Turf,'" Merlin says. "What is it?"

"Lobster and Steak," the server says.

"I'll have two of each."

The server doesn't bat an eye. It's the age of excess, after all. "We can do that."

"And you, ma'am?" the server asks Morgaine.

"Filet Mignon."

"How would you like your steak cooked?"

Morgaine folds her menu and looks straight at me. "Bloody."

Whoa. Okay. There! I nudge Merlin. Did he see that? What was *that* about? I totally sense hostility. And creeper vibes.

After the server leaves, I lean forward and lower my voice. "Does that mean you're plan to killing me?" An uncomfortable pause. "Again?"

By this point in our relationship, I'm comfortable enough to ask her.

"Of course not, Laurel."

"Not even a tiny bit?"

"Laurel..." She shakes her head. "I've told you once and I'll tell you again: I have more important things to do at the moment."

Hm.

That's what she told me during our ill-fated alliance in Regency England, and it ended with Morgaine hunting me through London on the back of Pepper, her pet pterodactyl. She had tried to zap me with her lightning hands, and I swore I'll never trust her again. Now I'm having an expensive WASP dinner with her in 1987.

Fool me once, right?

I'm no genius, but either Morgaine has unsavory things in store for me or she gets off on making me uncomfortable. Let's give her the benefit of the doubt. Maybe she just has one of those sociopathic faces. I mean, look at Merlin. He's smoking hot, but one glance at that chiseled mug and tell me if you don't plan to lock your doors at night.

Our food arrives.

Morgaine unfurls her napkin and sips her lemon water. "I like my meat *bloody*. Very bloody."

"That's nice, Morgaine," I say. "I don't know what that has to do with anything."

And then it happens. She peers at me over the rim of her glass and grins.

*Just grins. No blinking.*

I slump back in my seat and turn to Merlin. "Yeah, I'm totally dead. The question is: *when.*"

Merlin pats my hand. "At least she took you shopping."

## 7

"So how are we getting to Miami?" Vicky asks.

"We fly," Morgaine says.

"By plane or by pterodactyl?"

"Plane."

"What happened to Pepper?" Vicky glowers over the rim of her wineglass.

Morgaine clears her throat. "Pepper is back where she belongs and licking her wounds."

She glares at Merlin, who is partially responsible for Pepper's injury. Merlin's blameless. He was just trying to rescue us from Morgaine's pterodactyl attack. How else are you supposed to battle a dinosaur if not with a bigger dinosaur? Somehow Merlin got his hands on a T-Rex and Morgaine had her ass handed back to her. Pepper got hurt in the battle, something Merlin feels terrible about. Vicky's jimmy leg rocks the table. "I see you've given up shrinking people."

Morgaine sighs. "What's wrong, Vic?"

"Nothing's wrong," Vicky says with a sniff.

"Something's clearly wrong. You're mad at me."

"Huh. You're observant."

"Why are you mad? What did I do?"

"You should know what you did..."

I follow their argument like a tennis match. I'm a highly sensitive person—an empath. I don't like fights at dinner. It gives me flashbacks to family Thanksgivings and my parents bickering over burnt turkey. Merlin is blissfully oblivious and stuffing his face with steak and lobster.

"Is this about me shrinking you?" Morgaine asks. "That was an accident."

"Is that an apology?" Vicky snaps.

"Why should I apologize for something I didn't intentionally do? You got in the way of my target."

As Vicky's eyes widen, I toss down my napkin. That's my cue to leave.

"Come on, Merlin." I tug his arm.

He pokes his head up, still chewing. "But my supper!"

"We've gotta go. Now." I cock my head at Vicky and her furiously shaking leg. She's about to blow her top and I don't want to be in the blast zone.

"Oh." Merlin finally understands my cues. He forks one more bite of steak in his mouth and we scatter.

The servers bring out dessert, sherry, and port. Life is good for the Republicans of Sherman Oaks.

Darkness settles over the Valley and the stars cast a sparkling net over the mountains.

A lounge singer croons Frank Sinatra.

Elderly couples sway on the dance floor.

Men in clubhouse blazers puff on Cuban cigars and shit talk the U.S.S.R.

I eye Merlin. "Do you dance?"

"Dancing is for the court fool."

"Let your hair down a little," I say, holding out my hand. "You're in the '80s."

Merlin frowns. "My hair is down."

I tug him toward me. He stiffens as I wrap his arms around my waist and we gently sway next to the pool.

"This 'dancing' is not so terrible," Merlin says.

"It's not real dancing."

"What is real dancing?"

"Something that works up a sweat." The music and wine lulls me into tranquility. I rest my sleepy head against Merlin's shoulder. His linen Miami Vice jacket scratches my cheek. He smells like Aqua Net (we *all* smell like Aqua Net, so maybe I'm smelling myself?).

"I'm actually have a good time," I say, trying to keep my heavy eyelids open. "I love the '80's. No bloodthirsty mob. No tentacle monsters. No royal conspiracies. Just shopping and dining and free memberships into exclusive country clubs. I haven't checked my dying Instagram account or given my firing from Ainsley Mills a second thought. Dare I say it? I'm enjoying life."

I glance up at Merlin. He's staring straight ahead, his expression brooding (isn't it always?) and impassive. "I bet you haven't had time to worry about Arthur and his problems."

Merlin frowns.

"Have you?"

No answer.

"Hey!" I brighten up. "Why don't we hit up Vegas when we get back? I'll treat you to an All You Can Eat buffet and then we'll—"

"Laurel Kirby..." Sadness permeates his tone and softens his flinty eyes.

"What?"

"I cannot join you at the buffet." A pause. "What is a 'buffet'?"

"It's like the Great Hall banquet in Camelot, except with better food. Lobster, steak, sushi, unlimited salad options. All you can eat."

Merlin's eyes widen as he considers the possibilities. "When you say 'All you can eat'..."

"You can stay all night and butter your belly as you please, though I wouldn't advise it unless you want to gain two hundred pounds."

A struggle creeps across his face. He pulls away from me and curses under his breath. "I cannot join you."

*"What?"*

Merlin turn down food? Now I know something is wrong.

I blink. *"Why?"*

"After this adventure," he begins, "I will return to my time."

*"What?"*

I thought Merlin would stick around forever. He's having the time of his life in the future. I just figured he was sick of cleaning up Arthur's mess.

It never occurred to me that Merlin would *want* to go home.

A spike forms in my throat. "This is all so sudden. Are you sure?"

Merlin sighs. "There is much I have to do at Camelot. Arthur needs me."

I blink away my tears. "But I need you too. Who will take my picture?"

Merlin shudders at the mention of taking my photo. "You will find someone to torture. I am sure of it."

"So you're really going back?"

A solemn nod.

I lower my head. I don't know what to say. As much as I've complained about Merlin cramping my style, I've grown accustomed to his face. His smiles, his frowns... mostly his frowns. Merlin tips my chin up with his finger. "Why the onion-eye?"

"I'm going to miss you Merlin."

He draws me back in his arms. "I shall miss you too, Laurel Kirby."

I rest my cheek on his shoulder. I'm going to savor this night and enjoy Merlin's friendship for as long as I have it. Why do all good things have to come to an end?

"I thought we had at least nineteen adventures in us!"

"Where will we go?" He rests his chin on my head.

"Ancient Egypt. The Roaring Twenties. Or just back to my time. It doesn't matter where we are, just so long as..." Is this really happening? Merlin is actually leaving me? He's been a thorn in my side, a prick in my neck...

He's become my best friend.

What will I do without him?

Who's going to laugh at my jokes? Or in Merlin's case, *not* laugh at my jokes.

"We still have this adventure. Laurel Kirby, I..."

A scream, followed by a SPLASH, breaks our sentimental bubble. We whip our head around.

Vicky and Morgaine have jumped in the pool fully clothed. Vicky screams bloody murder and tries to drown Morgaine.

Morgaine splashes Vicky in the face and frog swims away.

I look up at Merlin. "I can't believe you want to give all this up."

## 8

MERLIN'S PLANS TO leave keeps me up all night. I'm grouchy during our flight to Miami. Good thing boarding a plane is super easy in 1987.

There's no TSA and you don't have to check in an hour early to board. You don't have to take off your shoes and walk through a metal detector, or else Morgaine would be screwed because she comes to the airport with twenty bangles on each wrist. She books us each first-class tickets. I'm overjoyed until we board. I sniff the cabin. Cigarette smoke?

Sure enough, the man behind me is chain-smoking up a storm, except, this being first class, he's puffing on a Cuban cigar.

My seat is next to Merlin. He demands the window seat. I shuffle down the aisle. There's no middle seat. We're in first class after all.

Vicky and Morgaine, still not speaking after last night's pool fight, are seated across the aisle from each other. Vicky flags down a flight attendant. "I thought this was a no smoking zone! I want to speak to the captain."

"Vicky's got her Asian Karen hat on." I spritz my face with

rose-scented mist and lean back, hoping Vicky doesn't get us thrown off the plane.

Midway through the flight, Merlin offers me his pretzels.

"Didn't you already have a lobster lunch?"

"Prawns."

"How much can you eat?"

"I can always eat." He empties the bag. "These pretzels are making me thirsty. May I have your drink?"

I scoot my gin and tonic away from Merlin's reach. "No!"

"You are in a foul mood."

"No, I'm not."

"Yes, you are. You are very prickly and your nostrils are flaring most unattractively." He peers at my profile, then notices my unopened bag of honey peanuts. "Are you going to eat those?"

I toss the bag in his lap, guzzle my cocktail, and yank down my sleeping mask. "Just leave me alone."

I can't get to sleep. I'm restless and sullen and I don't want to talk to anyone, least of all Merlin.

We're somewhere over Nebraska when I peel off my eye mask to look out the window. Merlin's head is slumped against my shoulder. He's snoring away without a care in the world. A ray of sunlight streams across his chiseled face. His dark lashes casts shadow spokes against his cheeks. The beginnings of a five o'clock shadow creeps across his jaw.

I sigh, unable to lift the heavy sadness from my heart. I can't believe he's leaving me! How selfish of him!

I suppose all good things must come to an end. Merlin can't hang with me forever. He's got responsibilities in Camelot. A court of dumb teenagers to advise, a Crusade to win. Whereas I...

What do I have? A dull job at a latex company (oh shit... I forgot to request vacation time). Okay. Strike that. A *former* dull job at a latex company and a short-lived stint as an influencer of some repute.

My eyes mist over. I blink back hot tears. This is why I never self-reflect. It opens up a depressing can of worms. I'm having another millennial life crisis. What do I do with my life? I'm drifting through life like a plastic bag floating through the wind... discarded by my followers, by a string of exes, and now Merlin.

Maybe I *should* take Morgaine up on her offer and rule England.

If I were important...

If I were queen...

Merlin will totally stick around. His job is to advise the monarch, right? I can be the monarch. It shouldn't be hard. I mean, if Arthur Pendragon (again, *badass* name) can do it...

What does King Arthur have that I don't have? I've pulled the sword from the stone *and* I didn't even need to make such a fuss about it. Excalibur belongs to me just as much as it does Arthur...

If I became queen, Merlin will have no choice but to stay.

Merlin cracks open an eye. "Were you watching me sleeping, Laurel Kirby?"

"Don't flatter yourself. I'm just... viewing the scenery."

He frowns and peers in my face. "Something is wrong."

"Why do you say that?" My voice rises an octave too high.

"That wrinkle on your forehead—"

I touch my forehead. Oh no. I have wrinkles now? How many wrinkles do I have? "What of it?"

"You only get that when you're thinking."

"I never think."

"I know. But occasionally you *do* think and nothing good comes of it."

Oh shit. He's onto me. I stand up. "I need to use the bathroom."

I scoot my way to Morgaine's seat and tap her on the shoulder. She's wide awake and reading *The Wall Street Journal*. Vicky is fast asleep behind her eye-mask.

I speak out of the corner of my mouth, making sure to keep my gaze fixed forward, "Come with me to the bathroom."

"I don't need to go."

"Yes. You. Do."

"I'm good."

I check over my shoulder. Merlin is ordering another in-flight meal.

"Trust me, Morgaine," I mumble-growl my words, "I have something to say that would be of *great* interest to you." *Cough.* "The throne of England?"

Morgaine's eyes light up. She discards her newspaper and stands up, smoothing down her mini skirt. "After you."

## 9

Morgaine is not happy about squeezing inside the tiny bathroom with me, even though it's the larger first class bathroom.

We crash into each other as the plane runs into a patch of turbulence.

Morgaine pinches her nose. "Smells like someone blew ass in here."

"I think the guy with the beer belly." I fight the urge to gag. "I think he had the salmon. Oh God, I think I'm going to puke."

"Hold on."

Morgaine waves her hand. The stink vanishes, replaced by a fresh spring meadow.

My nausea subsides. I inhale the floral scented air. "You've *got* to teach me how to do that!"

"Cut the crap, Laurel." Morgaine leans against the sink and folds her arms across her chest. "Why did you call me in here?"

This is it. The moment of truth.

I clasp my hands together. "I'm in."

"In what?"

Seriously? Some people can be so dense. "The Queen thing. I'm down with it. Let's do it! Let's conquer England."

Morgaine's sculpted eyebrows lift in surprise. "*You* want to be queen."

"Yup."

"You?"

I don't care for her skeptical tone. "Why not me? I pulled Excalibur from the stone, didn't I? I've proven that I'm just as worthy as Arthur and I'm twice as mature."

Morgaine rubs her temples like she's having trouble comprehending. "You've been so resistant, stubborn, apathetic, and stupid."

"Hey!"

"Why the sudden change of heart?" She tries to read my face. "Why now?"

My eyes shift to the side. "I care about England and the future of my people."

"No, you don't." She takes a step closer until we're nose to nose and peers into my eyes. Her brows furrow. My scalp begins to tingle.

Oh shit. Can she read minds? Is that a hidden sorceress power she hasn't revealed yet?

"You are a puzzle, Laurel Kirby," Morgaine says. "I can't seem to figure you out. What are you up to? What's going on in that tiny brain?"

*Tiny brain?* That's a little uncalled for, isn't it?

I train my face into an impassive mask. "Nothing." Technically, that isn't a lie. Right now I'm thinking about lunch. The in-flight menu doesn't look too bad, but the question is: do I have the Penne alla Vodka or the Salisbury steak?

"Why are you doing this?" Morgaine presses.

"I told you. I care about the welfare of my people."

"The English are not your people."

"Not true. I think we bonded during my vacation. And the

children! I'm doing it for the children because... children are the future?"

I can't tell her I'm doing this for a guy. She'll lose respect for me.

Morgaine's gaze is a hot lamp in a police interrogation room. Beads of perspiration drip from my temple. It's impossible to tell what she's thinking.

"Morgaine?" I gulp. "Speak to me."

She nods. "Okay."

"Okay?"

"I'm in."

"We're doing this? We're teaming up? Another royal takeover? Are we going to do it like last time?" I cringe. I'm not crazy about the idea of magically shrinking the royals. Since we're in the '80s, does that mean I'll have a tiny Prince Charles and Queen Elizabeth II on my hands?

"I haven't planned that far yet." Morgaine rubs her temple again. "I have a lot on my mind."

"Mordred."

"That boy has given me more grey hairs than I can count."

I get it. Morgaine's juggling a lot of plates. It's hard enough being an evil sorceress plotting world domination, let alone a single mother.

"So you don't have a plan?" I'm a little disappointed. The Morgaine I know is a multitasker. Guess the 'Mordred Situation' is getting to her.

"I'll come up with something in Miami," she says, sounding hassled.

"Cool. Okay. Operation Royal Takeover 2.0 is going to be *sweet*."

I still don't know how I feel about being queen (sounds like a lot of work). Whatever the outcome, I'll have Merlin's undivided attention.

"Good," I nod, "We're settled. You'll fill me in on the details and I'll plan my royal outfits."

I reach for the door.

Morgaine seizes my arm. "Not so fast. You've flaked out on me before."

*"Flaked?"* How dare she! What an accusation!

I don't recall flaking on... Oh. Right. The unpleasantness with King George, which led to Morgaine chasing us around London on her pterodactyl. "If I recall, you promised you weren't going to hurt our tiny captives. You broke your promise first. I just *reacted* to your lies by... running away."

"I'm going to need a contract going forward," Morgaine says.

"Good! I'll need a contract from *you*. How do we do this? Do we need a lawyer? I'll get Vicky to draft one up."

"That won't be necessary," Morgaine says, and my gaze flickers to the object in her hands. The Rubik's Cube I solved at the mall. She twists the cube, mix-matching the colors and erasing my work. "This contract is between you and me..."

"What contract?" I ask, expecting to see her produce a document for me to sign.

With another twist, the Rubik's Cube glows purple.

My eyes widen. I back away until I bump into the door. "What are you going to do with that?"

Morgaine practically shoves her enchanted Rubik's Cube in my face. "Touch the Cube."

"No!"

"Laurel... this is our binding agreement."

"I thought we were just going to sign some papers. Maybe E-Sign a PDF." I'm sweating bullets. My mouth is parched. "What are you going to do with that? Trap my soul in it?"

Silence.

Oh shit. Why do I always have to be right?

"It won't hurt." Morgaine takes a step closer. The neon glow cast a harsh shadow over her face until she resembles a sinister fortune teller. "There's already a piece of me in there."

I eye the Rubik's Cube. "When did you put yourself in there?"

"Last night."

"Gross! Why did you do that?!"

"Now all I need is a piece of you and then we're set."

"I don't want any part of myself mingling with you! You get my soul—"

"1/7th of your soul," she corrects. "A tiny sliver."

"I don't want you to have any of it! What do I get? Seems like you're getting the lion's share of the deal." I shake my head. "No, deal's off. I'm out."

I yank the latch and manage to pry the door open before it shuts in my face.

"You'll get 1/7 of my powers," Morgaine says.

I glance over my shoulders. "Seriously?"

Morgaine sounds pleased with herself. "Not such a bad deal, is it?"

I whirl around, my interest piqued. "Purple lightning hands? It's mine?"

"Lightning hands, yes. I can't predict what your 'soul color' will be."

No way! The soul comes in colors?

"The ability to shrink people?" I ask.

She nods.

"Flying?"

"I can't fly."

I arch my eyebrow. "Your cheekbones?"

Morgaine shrugs. "The possibilities are endless."

I purse my lips, weighing the pros and the cons of letting Morgaine 'borrow' my soul. This is *exactly* the type of devil's bargain I've been warned about in movies. On the other hand, it would be awesome to shoot lightning from my fingertips and move things with my mind. It's like having the Force except without all the Jedi training.

"Okay. I'm in."

Morgaine's grins. She holds out the enchanted Rubik's Cube.

"I can't believe I'm doing this." Squeezing my eyes shut, I touch the cube and a surge of purple light fills the first class bathroom.

———

A LONG LINE of disgruntled passengers sneer at us as we exit the bathroom.

I give the woman at the head of the line an apologetic shrug. "Sorry."

"Sorry." Morgaine apologizes to the entire line. She smooths down her mini skirt. I hoist up my push-up bra. Without meeting each other's eyes, we return to our seats.

"So how about that turbulence," I say, fanning myself. "Is it me or is it stuffy in here?"

Merlin studies me with his flinty gaze. "You were gone for a long time."

"My period."

"Why did Morgaine join you?"

"Is this an interrogation?"

Merlin stares me down. He's really good at that. He just stares and stares with those dark, suspicious, judgmental eyes. No words. No blinking. Why doesn't he blink? Doesn't his eyes get dry?

I shrink down in my seat.

"Look, if you *have* to know... I ran out of tampons and Morgaine lent me some. They're hard to, you know, insert and—"

Merlin holds up his hand. "No more."

"Then it got stuck and she had to dive in deep — "

He shakes himself like a wet dog. "I wished I never asked."

I settle back, smug. *That's* how you play the woman card.

Afterward, Merlin is too distracted by the in-flight movie (*Dirty Dancing* projected on a screen at the front of the plane) to pay any more attention to me. I order Chicken a la King and a Long Island Iced Tea. I'm feeling good about this contract and, actually, I feel perfectly normal until...

I pick up my fork. A zing of electricity courses through my bloodstream. I tingle and twitch.

Out of the corner, I catch Merlin watching me.

"What was that?" he asks.

"What?" I wiggle in my seat.

"That."

"Oh, you know," I massage my stomach, "checking for leakage."

Wrinkling his nose in discomfort, Merlin focuses on the movie and forgets all about me.

I ball up my hands and sit on them, hiding the hot pink sparks zinging through my nails.

## 10

I can't believe I'm a sorceress!

Technically, 1/7th a sorceress, but that's better than nothing. I have Morgaine's magic powers and I can't wait to see what I can do. The possibilities are endless.

I can ZAP anyone of my choosing, except, it's a dick move to obliterate someone with lightning hands.

Having been the target of Morgaine's lightning hands, I'd say that shit *hurt*.

I'll only ZAP someone in self-defense. Or if I witness a bank robbery, car jacking, mugging... Criminals beware! After all, with great power comes great responsibility.

We've landed in Florida and I'm bursting with excitement as we cruise down Ocean Drive in a Ferrari convertible.

As horrible a person as Morgaine is, one thing I have to say in her favor: she travels in style. Other than the brief unpleasantness of pouring 1/7th of my soul in her enchanted Rubik's Cube, I'm having a great time in 1987. No complaints here!

Merlin and I lounge in the backseat.

I'm gawking at the pastel buildings and neon signs.

Palm trees line the sidewalk and the beach is a stone's throw away.

Now *this* is what time travel is all about! To think, I've been freezing my ass off in England when I could have been working on my tan.

Next to me, Merlin seems to have the same idea. He lowers his RayBan Wayfarers and checks out two women in high-cut bikinis.

His mouth twitches. "I love Miami."

"Why would you ever want to go back to England?"

He doesn't answer, but continues to gawk at the busy sidewalk.

A heady mixture of roast pork, tropical flowers, mojitos, and coconut sunscreen perfumes the air. I drape my arm across the backseat and tip my head back, soaking in the sun.

"Two rights and a left!" Vicky commands from shotgun. "The El Picante Hotel should be on the corner."

"Well, it's not," Morgaine says.

Vicky consults her map. "You took two lefts instead of a right..."

"Impossible. I know my left and my right."

"Do you, Morgaine? Do you really?"

"Check the map again."

"I'm checking it," Vicky jabs the map so hard she almost pokes her finger through the paper, "and it's two blocks west of Ocean Boulevard... *Goddamn it, Laurel! Stop kicking my seat!*"

"No feet on the leather," Morgaine snaps. "This is a rental."

"Alright. Alright. Geez!" I tuck my legs up to my chest.

"Laurel!" Morgaine eyes me in the rearview mirror. "Get your damn dirty feet off that seat. Look how well-behaved Merlin is. Why can't you be more like him?"

"Like him?" I turn to Merlin, who shoots me a smug smile. "All he does is eat and ogle hot babes!"

"But he's quiet and respects the leather," Vicky says. "Your feet are still on the seat."

Morgaine half swivels around. "Don't make me come back there..."

How can I soak in the sun and enjoy a tranquil car ride with these banshees bickering at each other and telling me what to do? It's like having *two* moms.

Vicky's taken it upon herself to navigate our mini road trip. We're looking for Mordred, who does not want to be found. All this time I assumed we were going to drop by his apartment and shake him up (that's when I use my lightning hands). As I later discovered, Mordred ditched his apartment a year ago.

Morgaine insists he's in Miami. She has reason to believe he's hiding out at El Picante Hotel, a seedy place off Miami's main drag.

We round a busy corner of beach-goers ready to cross the street.

"Let's ask for directions," Vicky suggests.

Morgaine waits for the pedestrians to cross before turning the corner. "I'm not asking for directions. I know exactly where the hotel is."

"Have you been before?"

"No."

"Then you don't know."

"I know." Morgaine picks up her gigantic car phone and punches in a number.

Vicky narrows her eyes. "Who are you calling?"

"My sources."

"What sources? I thought you worked alone."

"There are a lot of things you don't know about me," Morgaine says.

Vicky crosses her arms over her chest. "You've got that right."

I level Merlin with an exasperated look. They've been bickering all through the flight and car ride. It's ruining our vacation.

"I'm getting major family vacation flashbacks," I mutter under my breath.

Merlin frowns. "Family vacation?"

"You know, when you pile into a station wagon and take a trip to the Grand Canyon, eat greasy hamburgers, and crank up the music in your headphones while your parents bicker in the front seat?"

Merlin gawks at me with a blank stare. Given Merlin's life experiences, I might as well be speaking a foreign language. He doesn't have station wagons or greasy diner food in the Dark Ages.

He lived in a cave during his formative years and trained with an old sorcerer—much like a Jedi Knight — who expected him to practice his sorcery, carry buckets of water from the well, and never take vacations. His childhood sucked.

"Oh shit. I'm such a bonehead. You don't have parents. And here I am, acting like an insensitive prick, poking at your emotional wounds."

Merlin shrugs off my apology. "The Merlin is *here* now. I would like to go where all the naked people are."

"You want to go to the beach?"

"Aye."

"Can you swim?"

He levels me with a look that says, *'Come on. What do you think?'*

"Well, how am I supposed to know? England's oceans are cold. Did you swim in them as part of your wizard training?"

Merlin keeps his mouth shut. His side-eye tells me I've hit the nail on the head.

"Did you swim a triathlon?" I ask. Do *I* have to swim a triathlon now that I'm technically a sorceress? "What are we waiting for? The beach is literally *that* way. Yo Morgaine!" I tap the back seat. "Let's take a detour!"

"Are you *kidding* me?"

Geez. Was it something I said?

"We're on a mission to find my son," Morgaine says.

"Seriously, Laurel... " Vicky glares at me over her shoulder. "This is a *rescue* mission. Not a vacation."

Why can't it be both? Just because they're miserable doesn't mean Merlin and I have to be.

"Wherever Mordred is, I'm sure he can wait a few hours. We're only in '80's Miami once, right? And Merlin informs me he's leaving after this trip."

"So?" they both say.

Seriously, sometimes I think Morgaine and Vicky have a hive mind.

The car stops at a light. Morgaine whirls around. "Listen Laurel," she says in a 'don't make me turn this car around' tone, "I don't want to hear anymore whining."

"Two hours! *Come on*. Two... okay, one hour. Mordred can take care of himself for one measly hour... Hey, why don't you find the hotel and text me." I eye her enormous car phone. "Or call me. Merlin and I will meet up with you."

Morgaine sighs.

Good. She's weakening. I can tell she wants some peace and quiet. She's annoyed by me—has been annoyed by me since we first met. Our personalities don't mesh well.

"I don't know..." She casts me a suspicious look in the rearview mirror.

"I'm not backing out of our deal," I say, offended that the thought would even cross her mind. "Besides," I lower my voice and meet her gaze, "Remember the Rubik's Cube. You'll always know where I am."

"What's this about a Rubik's Cube?" Merlin asks.

"Yeah," Vicky says, "why did you whisper when we can totally hear you?"

"I didn't whisper. I just lowered my voice to an appropriate volume."

Morgaine points her finger at me. "*One* hour. I want you back in one hour and not a minute later."

I smile, victorious, and hop out of the convertible. "Thanks, Mom. You two stay out of trouble!"

Vicky glowers after me. She's just salty she can't enjoy the beach.

"What was that about?" Merlin falls in step beside me on our way to freedom.

"What was what about?"

"That look between you and Morgaine."

"Look? What look?"

"You shared a look," he says.

I laugh a little too loudly. "I look people in the eye when I talk to them. It's called manners."

Merlin considers my explanation with a skeptical tilt of his head. "Something is different about you," he grumbles. "Ever since you left the bathroom in the airplane."

My heart jolts in alarm. "What do you mean?"

"I can't put my finger on it."

I feel him studying my profile and look the other way. "Look! A cafe. Do you want to drop by for some iced coffee before — "

"You look different. You're starting to resemble... Morgaine."

"You mean my cheekbones?" I flaunt my right cheek. "She taught me how to contour."

"Hmm," he says. "Maybe. Nevertheless, I've got my eye on you, Laurel Kirby."

I halt before we reach the sand. "*You've* got *your* eye on *me*? Who do you think you are? Magnum P.I.?"

"I suspect you've been influenced." Merlin narrows his eyes. "*Badly* influenced by that blasted le Fey."

As MUCH AS I'd like to work on my tan, Merlin and I do not have time to lounge on the beach.

We're on a time limit. One hour to pack in all the beach action before Morgaine loses her shit.

I resent Morgaine for keeping us on such a tight leash. Merlin and I are both adults (Merlin is thousands of years old!) but Morgaine treats us like children. She's such a control freak! Leave it to her to put us on a strict Miami itinerary.

We haul ass to the docks. "Have you ever been on a jet ski?" I ask Merlin. "Wait. What am I asking? Of course you haven't! Where are you going to find jet skies at Camelot?"

Merlin turns the tables on me. "Have *you* ever been on a jet ski?"

"No! It's a first time for me too!"

I march up to the rental booth. "Two jet skies, please."

The transaction is a piece of cake. They never asked for ID or proof of age. For a moment, I was afraid they'd have to call Mommy and Morgaine will have to come here and sign for us. I have a gut feeling Morgaine wouldn't want us doing extreme water sports.

Strangely enough, I've conjured up a crystal clear image of Morgaine.

Morgaine's disembodied head, anyway. She's floating inches away from my face and looks so real I can reach out and touch her. Her body has been masked off like a bad Photoshop job and she's surrounded by a flashing neon prism. The purple neon accentuates her cheekbones and makes her look like an uber villain.

"This is an accident waiting to happen," she says. Synth pop music accompanies her criticism. It's a major production.

"Whoa!" I jump backward.

Merlin, who up until this point, has been studying the texture of sand (not a lot of sand in England. Lots of pebbles though...), rushes to my side. "Laurel Kirby! What is wrong?"

I point to the sorceress-prism-head in front of me. "Do you see that?"

"See what?"

"That!"

He squints at air. "I don't see anything." He touches my forehead. "You are not fevered."

Merlin tugs me beneath the shade of a palm tree and coaxes me to sit down in the sand.

"He can't see me," Morgaine says. Her voice is echo-y, like she's speaking to me in Superman's Cave of Solitude.

"Oh dear God!" I jump. "Did you hear that?"

"Hear what?" Merlin asks.

"As I told you before our pact," Morgaine says, "this is between you and me."

"This isn't happening." I draw my legs up to my chest and huddle. "I'm hallucinating because I'm dehydrated. I'm in a fugue state."

"Use your mind's voice," Morgaine says, "People are going to think you're crazy if you go around talking to yourself."

"I—" I glance into Merlin's concerned face.

"Get rid of him," she says.

"But I—"

"Mind-voice!"

"Merlin..." I lick my dry lips and choose my words carefully. "There's a bar at the corner. Can you get me some water?"

He drinks in my distress. "Whatever you need, Laurel Kirby."

I wait for Merlin to disappear before training the full force of my fury on Morgaine. "What the actual *fuck* is going on here?"

"Think it. Don't say it."

Me. Thinking: *"What's going on here?"*

"I can't hear you. You're mumbling. Think louder."

I roll my eyes. "How do I turn up the volume on my thoughts... oh wait. Here it is!"

"Too loud!"

Thoughts. Dialed down to an indoor volume: "Will nothing please you?"

"Better," she says.

"Cut the crap, Morgaine! Why are you in my mind?"

"You let me in."

"I *what*?"

"Remember our pact? 1/7th of your soul allows me access to 1/7th of your mind."

I gasp. "You can read my thoughts?"

"Only the thoughts you broadcast to me," she says. "And I can see what you do."

"You have access to my eyes?!" I swivel around. "What am I looking at now?"

"A couple strolling across the beach."

I curse. "And now?"

"A crushed Coke can half buried in the sand." Morgaine shakes her disembodied head. "I hate litter bugs."

"I know, right?! Like would it be too hard to walk your trash to the trash can?" I rub my temple. "I don't know about this. It's super invasive."

It's similar to when you download an app and it requests access to your phone's camera and microphone. First MorgVPN, now Morg Spyware. Morgaine has hacked my mind!

"Morg Spyware?" Morgaine says. "I like that. Mind if I use it?"

"You were listening in?"

"What do you think?"

"Wait... does this work both ways? Do I have access to your mind? And your eyes?"

"It's possible," Morgaine says. "But I've blocked you."

"There's nothing you're thinking that's interesting, anyway. How do I block you?"

Morgaine would be shrugging if she wasn't a disembodied head. "Figure it out."

Okay. I can see I'm not going to get any help from Morgaine. "What's the point of all this? So you can keep tabs on me? Ruin my fun? Helicopter parent much?"

Morgaine sighs. "I'm not your mother. You can do what you want, but if you should *ever* betray me like you did in London..."

"Yeah, yeah." My head bobs along. "This is insurance against betrayals." I consider her neon border and synthpop background music. "What's with the prism?"

"That's my Morg Spyware skin."

My eyes widen. "*What*? You can change skins?!?! What's my skin look like?"

"You're on default mode. Just a plain head."

"How do I change it?"

Morgaine walks me through the customization options of our soul pact. Leopard patterns accompanied by jungle horns. Nah. A floral crown. Oooh. This one smooths out my skin and thickens my lashes. Oooh, this one has cute sparkle hearts. I can't decide.

"JUST CHOOSE ONE ALREADY!"

"Okay, Okay." I select the floral crown skin and pair it with a gentle lute quartet. I might change the music later when I'm not feeling so hurried.

Merlin returns with my water, two shot glasses, and a cup full of lime wedges.

"Since when did you learn about tequila shots?"

"They are better than mead." Merlin whirls around and stares right at Morgaine's big giant head. "I sense something strange afoot."

He cannot see Morgaine, but he senses her presence.

I raise my tequila shot. "To the jet skis!" We clink glasses.

"Drinking and jet skiing?" Morgaine asks. "I wouldn't if I were you."

"Well, you're not me!"

"Laurel!"

"Bye, Mom."

I end the connection. "Ready, Merlin?"

He hesitates and cocks his head to a group also renting jet skis. Bikinis and swim trunks are the wardrobe of the day. He glances down at our clothes. "We are not dressed like the others."

He's right. He can't go into the water in his linen suit. My acid wash denim jumpsuit, decorated with geometric enamel pins, will only get ruined by the salt water.

I gaze around our little section of shade. We're far enough away from the beachcombers. With seconds of privacy to spare, it all depends on my speed.

"I can fix that," I say.

"How?"

How did Morgaine do this again? Magic isn't so hard. It shouldn't be harder than say... pulling Excalibur from the stone or solving a Rubik's Cube in three seconds flat.

A surge of electricity zips through me and collects at my fingertips. I'm hot to trot. If I touch Merlin, he'll light up like a pinball machine.

"With our powers combined," I say, snapping my fingers.

12

---

Oh shit.

I did it!

Merlin's in lime green swim trunks (Hey. Don't @ me. Gotta keep with the '80s aesthetics) and his abs are... Chef's kiss. *Double chefs kiss.* I don't know how he acquired a six-pack in the Dark Ages. Unless he began his day with a hundred crunches, the chiseled abs make no sense. During my stay in Camelot, I don't recall a gym or fitness center, unless you count the rack and various unsavory torture devices in the dungeon.

But I digress. Are we really here to ogle Merlin's *stacked* chest?

I've magicked myself a hot pink bikini with neon green straps and okay... I cheated. I know the '80s high cut bottoms are in, but I've been lax in my grooming if you know what I mean. So I gave myself a hipster-cut bottom. Gotta cover up the wilderness.

"I've got sunblock." I squeeze a dollop of lotion and advance on Merlin.

Merlin steps back, his eyes wide and wild. He's the definition of shook. "I knew it!"

"You knew what?" I rub sunblock on my shoulder.

"Morgaine got to you! I knew something happened in the bathroom."

Okay. So it may not be the brightest idea to flex my new magic powers in front of Merlin. He's tripping out and I'm not certain he's digging his new swim trunks.

Look at it from my angle: how would you feel if you got the coolest birthday present ever and can't show it off to your friends?

"Morgaine didn't 'get' to me."

"Then how do you explain the new clothes?"

I scoff. "I have a very good explanation."

Merlin glares down at me with his terrifying scowl. "Which is?"

Okay. Don't panic. Merlin is really grilling me here. Don't let him intimidate you. He wants an answer. Remember... The best lies stick to the truth.

"Well, if you want to know," I say, "I picked up some magic tricks from Morgaine a-a-and... you."

"Me? I never taught you magic."

"You didn't need to. I watched... and I learned."

"You watched Morgaine?"

"Morgaine? Please! Lightning hands? Tentacle monsters? Not to mention our girl's trip to London. You think she 'bought' our Regency wardrobe?" I tap my temple. "Eyes like a hawk."

Merlin takes in my claim of expert observation with a stroke of his chin. "Usually magic requires years—*decades* of study."

I flip my hair. "Like it's hard."

"The pupil must possess a proclivity toward—"

"Who pulled Excalibur from the stone?"

He plunges into another pensive silence. He knows I'm right. "I suppose you *did* solve that Rubik Cube faster than me."

I haven't even thought of that! Now that he's mentioned it, I might as well roll with it. "Seriously, Merlin. When will you stop underestimating me?"

"Laurel Kirby," Merlin lowers his head in shame, "I am humbled."

He's falling for it. He's *actually* falling for it!

Calm down. Be cool. Go with the flow. I gesture to our tubular (that's an '80s term, right?) jet ski rentals. "Let's ride some waves!"

13

Bright sun, blue skies, cool breeze, and sic waves. No, wait! It's the '80's: *Tubular* waves.

Now this is what I'm talking about! "Whoooooooo!" The wind is in my hair, salt water sprays my face, and the Miami skyline beckons from the shore.

Merlin and I are riding our jet skies like we stole them. Life is good and I don't have a care in the world. I'm not obsessed with my Likes and follower count—though this *would* be a great time for photos. I'm an influencer on the decline and you know what? I don't care. I'm *actually* grabbing life by the balls and living it up without the need to prove I'm having fun.

"Yo Merlin!" I call above the roar of my engine. "Figure eights!"

I slice through the water, criss-crossing around Merlin until we meet and power down our motors.

We high five.

"Don't you love this?" I ask.

"I enjoy Miami." His tone is as robotic as ever.

Merlin could use a little more excitement here.

"It's the most chill trip through time we've ever had." I search his face meaningfully. "There can be more fun trips through time," I say, wiping water from my face. "If you stay."

Merlin's carefree expression becomes serious again. "Laurel Kirby, you know I cannot."

"Why not?" I whine.

"I have responsibilities in my own time."

Here he goes again! He's a broken record.

"Why would you want to go back to a dank castle and deal with a dumb king, not to mention handle the serfs when you can have jet skies, sunshine, and tequila shots?"

Merlin scowls. "Arthur is not dumb."

I level him with a 'get serious' look. "We're talking about the same kid who banged his own sister."

"I concede he does not have his wits about him, but the king is still young and his intelligence will grow in time. I have pledged my fealty and am sworn to guide him through his rule."

This 'loyalty' business is really screwing up our time traveling partnership.

"You may return with me," Merlin suggests, reading my disappointment.

My head pokes up. "You want me to go with you? Back to Camelot?"

"The court will need an influencer and..." Merlin breaks eye contact and stares out into the vast ocean. "I will enjoy your company."

Wait. What is he saying here? He'll 'enjoy' my company? Is that his subtle way of saying he needs me too? Needs me for what? Friendship or sex? Would I be going out on a limb here to wonder if Merlin even has sex? I've worn seriously cute outfits around him and he hasn't checked me out once. He hasn't even checked out my ass in this bikini, which brings me to the conclusion that Merlin, in addition to living like a Medieval monk, is asexual. Tragic, isn't it? Maybe years of magic study wiped all the libido out of him.

Back to the matter at hand: go with Merlin? To Camelot? No. Oh, *hell* no. I may be living in a royal castle, but I like running water and flush toilets and being able to walk through town without judgmental serfs calling me a witch.

"Merlin, I—"

A horrified scream.

We whip our heads toward the shore. Water froths and stirs as hysterical swimmers make a mass exodus for land. It's like a scene from *Jaws* and sure enough, someone screams "Shark!"

We squint at the water. I spot an enormous fin barreling straight toward a group of children treading water. The fin is joined by a second, a third...

Oh shit. A school of sharks! All torpedoing toward the terrified children, who are too far out for rescuers at shore to reach in time. I meet Merlin's eyes. "The children!"

"They will be eaten," he says matter-of-factly.

That's Merlin for you. Always doom and gloom.

"Not on my watch!" I rev up my jet ski and blast through the waves.

I'm pushing my jet ski to the limit, hauling ass to scoop up the swimmers before they become lunch.

The sharks circle the victims, cutting off their escape route.

"Help!"

"Help!"

"Call the coast guard!" says the frantic spectators on shore.

The coast guard won't get here in time. Good thing I'm here. I AM THE COAST GUARD.

I ready my sorceress hands and think angry thoughts:

Morgaine putting me in a chokehold.

Morgaine hacking into my Instagram and posting unaesthetic photos of me, causing me to lose followers.

Buying the wrong kind of printer paper at work and getting torn a new one.

Vicky's bitchy face.

I don't know the ins and outs of sorcery, but it's working! My juices are flowing. Angry thoughts ignite a spark. Electricity surges through me. I'm a lightning rod, baby! Can't touch this.

I power slide close enough to see the first shark's black doll eyes as it zeros in for the kill. While the other sharks are normal shark-size, their leader is part whale. She's the biggest fish I've ever seen — twenty feet if she was a foot. A Great White out to do some serious damage.

"Nope!" I wax circles in the air with my sorceress hands. As the Great White's razor-sharp teeth prepares to chomp down on a leg, I attack.

ZAP!

A neon pink fishing net springs from my fingers and wraps around the shark, suspending it in midair.

Whoa! I didn't even know I can conjure up nets. My net is charged with electricity. The shark's slippery body shakes like I'm frying it up on the grill and her beady black eyes roll to the back of her head. I sniff the air and my stomach growls. It smells like a fish fry. *If you squeeze some lemon on...*

No! I will not think about eating this shark.

*Some tartar sauce would...* No!

The other sharks sense the vibrations in the water. Can sharks be shook?

One by one, the shark gang retreats.

I hold the alpha shark hostage in my magic snare. My hands tremble with the effort. Who knew sorceress magic could be so draining?

"Hurry children!" I grit my teeth. "I don't know how much longer I can hold it."

Merlin power slides next to me and watches my lightning hands at work. "Are you sure you learned this through observation? This is magic of the highest caliber: too advanced for the likes of you."

Seriously? I'm up to my elbows in Great White and he's heckling me? "Merlin, you're not helping."

"I do not believe your lies. You cannot have learned this by watching Morgaine. You're always on your phone."

A surge of anger zips through my body. I blip for just a second. My fury is white hot.

The shark spazzes out in my electric-fishing net, shook but not hurt.

Pink lasers flashes, followed by an unexpected... sonic BOOM.

Oh God.

A geyser of bloody water shoots to the sky. Shark chunks blow through the air.

The horror! The horror!

I lower my hands, mortified. "I blew it up," I squeak. "I blew up the shark!"

The spectators on shore let out a collective "Ewwwwww."

There's a moment of silence. Heads turn in our direction.

Fingers point at me. "She did it!"

"I saw her do it!"

"She blew up the shark."

A roar of disgust.

"She's a shark killer."

*"Shark killer!"*

*"Shark killer!"*

Surfers grab their boards.

Two guys on Sea-Doos rev up their engine.

"Get her!"

"Get the shark killer!"

*Oh shit.* My stomach bottoms out. It's the serf/Regency gentleman mob all over again.

"I didn't mean to kill the shark!" My excuse earns a backlash of disgust.

I turn to Merlin. "Quick! Show me how to put him back together again."

"It doesn't work that way. Once you've killed, you cannot un-kill."

"Merlin! You're no help! I can totally put the shark back together. Lemme think. I can—" I grit my teeth as a sharp ringing pierces my eardrums.

Morgaine's purple prism face materializes before me. "WHAT DID YOU DO?"

## 14

Multi-tasking comes in handy at times like these. I'm grateful I had such a hectic day job at the latex company. Going on coffee runs while styling latex for a photo shoot *and* fixing the busted printer isn't for the faint of heart. While I may complain about being too busy to breathe at that job, it's nothing compared to the sheer disaster I have to handle now. In fact, it's prepared me for my current situation.

"They're gaining on us!" I shout above the roar of my jet ski. Wind whips my hair like a banner in the wind. Saltwater sprays my face and stings my eyes.

"We have the upper hand!" Merlin keeps pace beside me as we slice through the waves.

A speed boat joins our Sea-Doo pursuers. Men in mirrored sunglasses and baseball caps holler obscenities at us. The speed boat guys chuck empty beer cans at our backs.

"Shark killer!"

Geez. I killed *one* shark. I was only trying to help. It was an accident and I feel horrible about it.

Maybe we should talk about how these sharks could have massacred a bunch of kids if I hadn't intervened. Or let's talk about how my pursuers are treating the ocean like a landfill. Litter kills more aquatic life than magic ever could.

"You make a good point. I abhor littering." Morgaine's disembodied head continues to bob before me. "The first logical thought you've had since I've known you."

I honestly can't do this right now. Not only am I being pursued by drunken Sea-Doo mercenaries hell bent on citizen's arrest, Morgaine has been nagging me the entire time. It's hard concentrating on a jet ski chase while your arch nemesis heckles you about 'irresponsible use of powers' and shames you for 'revealing yourself to the masses.'

As the Sea-Doo guys close in, my jet ski sputters. I. Do. Not. Need. This. Right. Now.

What did I do? Cook the motor? Run out of gas? I've pushed my jet ski to the limit.

I check over my shoulder. Goddamn! Sea-Doos are fast.

"Seems like you've lost the upper hand," Morgaine says.

"A little help here?"

"No, I don't think I will. You've made your bed. Now lie in it."

Omigod. Morgaine is like the coldest bitch ever. I don't know why I keep giving her second chances.

"Okay," I snap. "You can go now."

"Actually, I prefer to stick around and watch."

"Seriously?! You're such an asshole." I check on Merlin. His jet ski is smoking and sputtering too. "Where do we go from here?"

Our original plan—and it wasn't much of a plan—was to ride into the distance or until our pursuers tire. Problem is: the ocean is vast and our jet skies only have so much range. Our pursuers are like super motivated to enact stupid justice on me. Cue hillbilly chase music: Aqua edition.

"I've got the Shark Killer! Let's beat her up."

Whoa.

That's a little harsh, isn't it? I thought they were only going to turn me over to the coast guard.

My jet ski squirts a puff of black smoke and jolts to a dead halt. Sea water splashes my legs.

Merlin comes up behind me. "Hop on!"

I have no choice. I have to jump. I stand on my seat, arms wide open, knees bent... "I'm ready!"

Merlin gives me a thumbs up.

I leap frog in the air (praying all the while) and land behind him. "Gah!" I bang up my shins pretty badly.

"Are you hurt?" He asks over his shoulder.

I grit my teeth. "I don't need my legs, anyway. Go! Go! Go!"

Morgaine's big smug face laughs. "Impressive. You're more entertaining than a bad action movie."

You know what? I don't need to listen to this. I crank up the music *in my mind* to a mix of '80s power ballads (apt music for a Miami jet ski chase, don't you think?) and crank up the volume.

Morgaine is displeased at being muted. Tough shit. Now I can concentrate on the problem at hand: Merlin's jet ski is slowing down.

A beer can pelt me in the back.

"Ow!" I glare over my shoulder.

"Whoooooooo!" My attacker pumps his fist in the air. "Got her!"

"Look! They're out of gas," says his friend with the douchy gold sunglasses. "Now we can beat her up!"

"Pedal to the metal, Merlin!"

Merlin cranks her up to full throttle. His jet ski is like an exhausted mule, creaking along in a sputter of acrid smoke. Water sloshes our laps.

Another beer can bounce off my head.

"Ow!" I whirl around, sorceress hands at the ready.

"Refrain from magic, Laurel Kirby," Merlin says. "You don't know your own strength!"

He's right. I've already blown up a shark today. The last thing

I need is a mass murder on my list of screw-ups. I lower my hands, shamed. "Do something! They're gaining on us."

"I am trying!"

"Try harder!"

One of the fishing boat guys perches on the prow. He's swinging a fishing net.

My eyes widen. "Oh *hell* no!"

Just as he's about to launch the net at us, a blast of water knocks him back. Another splash thwarts the Sea-Doo dudes' advance.

I shield my eyes.

A sleek white cigarette boat power slides in front of us in all its high tech glory. The boat's name, painted in rad blue and purple '80s letters, reads "Tiger Blood."

The cigarette boat comes to a full stop. The captain hops on the prow. He's a dashing guy in his early '20s, dressed in head to toe white.

His shirt is unbuttoned at the neck, revealing three massive gold chains. His hair is dark and sleek, extremely oily and styled in a... I don't want to say mullet. It's more like a half-mullet. A baby mullet. Gross, but not as gross as it *could* be.

I can't see his eyes behind his mirrored aviator shades, but his cheekbones are prominent and enviable, hollowed into a permanent Blue Steel.

He bends down and lends me a hand. "Come with me if you want to live," he says, his mouth curled into a cocky grin.

"Who are you?" My eyes narrow in suspicion. Something about this guy seems very familiar.

"You don't remember me?" My flashy rescuer whips off his shades, revealing intense blackish eyes much like his mother's.

I gasp. "Mordred?"

## 15

I'm BARELY over the side of Mordred's fancy boat before the Sea-Doos are back in business. They've opened up another six-pack of beer. *Oh shit.* Stocking up on ammo.

"Shark killer! Shark killer! Shark killer!"

Their words become more and more slurred with each beer guzzled. I'm not worried of immediate attack.

Mordred drapes an arm over my shoulder and guides me behind the wheel. "Come sit beside me, baby," he says, his gaze roving over my bikini-clad body.

*Baby?*

Well... Okay. Not sure how I feel about Baby Mordred calling *me* baby. His arm slides to my waist. Okay. Whoa. Mordred is friendly. A little *too* friendly. As his hand dips lower, I ease myself away before he could grope my butt.

I'll give Mordred the benefit of the doubt solely because I knew him as a cute infant. He's probably starved for affection. Is it any wonder with Morgaine as his mother? Who knows what psychological damages she could have inflicted upon him over the years.

"They are very enthusiastic, yes?" Mordred watches my

pursuers work themselves into a drunken frenzy. "It is fun to watch. That one in the red hat reminds me of a beaver. He is very funny. Very funny indeed."

His laughter doesn't meet his eyes, which is *such* a Morgaine trait.

I don't think it's very funny. "Except this beaver is out for blood. *My* blood! How can you be so calm about these assholes? They have us surrounded."

Mordred whips out a comb and tends to his half-mullet. "It is not a problem."

Is it me or does Mordred sound like an international B movie villain? You know, the guy in the white suit and fake tan with a cigar clamped between his teeth as he machine guns down his enemies from a chopper?

Merlin climbs over the cigarette boat, mumbling about how he could've used a hand too.

"Merlin!" I jump up and greet my forgotten companion. "It's Mordred. All grown up! Remember when you held him as a baby?"

"How can I forget!" Mordred welcomes Merlin aboard his boat with arms wide open. "Uncle Merlin!"

"Uncle?" I mouth as Mordred smooches Merlin on both cheeks and gives him a giant bear hug.

Merlin eyes me for help. He's stiff and he looks like he desperately wants to pry Mordred off of him.

At last, Mordred pulls away, his eyes sparkling with merriment. "I am happy to see you, Uncle!"

Merlin blinks in surprise. "Are you?"

"Yes! You are family." He draws me into the group hug. "We are *all* family."

Merlin and I exchange a quizzical look.

Mordred has grown up to be a charming young man. Handsome, affectionate... I wiggle away as he tries to grope my ass again. Maybe he could dial down the affection a notch or two. I gaze around the fancy cigarette boat with its state-of-the-art marine radio and supple leather seats.

I don't know why Morgaine thinks Mordred's fallen in with the wrong crowd. He seems like an upstanding character to me. A bit on the touchy side, but not the loser drug addict she's painted him out to be.

"It's a good thing you found us, Mordred," I say. "We were looking for you."

"Looking for me?" His eyes light up. It's amazing how much he resembles Morgaine, but he's also inherited the classic golden boy handsomeness of his father, King Arthur. Who says inbreeding produces ugly babies? Baby Mordred is, dare I say it, hot. He needs to do something about the half-mullet, though.

"We came to Miami with your mother. She's worried sick."

At the mention of Morgaine, a storm cloud shadows Mordred's charming facade. He scowls. "What does that witch want now?"

"Mordred! That's a horrible way to refer to your mother!" Though he has a point: Morgaine sucks in many ways.

"She thinks you're mixed up with a bad crowd. I think you're doing just fine."

"Hey shark killer!" One of the my attackers calls, "Eat shit!"

A beer can sails into the boat. I dodge the missile and it hits Mordred between the shoulder blades. He straightens up and checks over his shoulders. "Big mistake, my friends." His words are cool, his meaning deadly. "Big mistake."

He jams two fingers into his mouth and whistles. Two rough-looking characters emerge from below deck.

Merlin and I jump back. Whoa. "Where'd those guys come from?"

Whoever they are, I wouldn't want to run into them in a dark alley. The bigger of the two is built like a brick shithouse and looks like he could bench press a tank. In contrast, the smaller of the two is whip thin, has a slick ponytail thing going on (the only

'80s men's hairstyle worse than a mullet) and resembles a human weasel.

"You whistled, boss?" Weasel asks. I exchange another confused look with Merlin. "Boss?" I mouth.

Mordred cocks his head toward the drunks. "Take care of this garbage, yes?"

"Right away, Boss."

Brick Shithouse grunts. They disappear below deck again and emerge with M-16s.

"Whoa."

Okay. I said I was shook before, but this is the *most* shook I've ever been. And to put things into perspective, I've witnessed a *dinosaur* battle in London.

Brick Shithouse bumps into Merlin and doesn't apologize. The two men size each other up like pro wrestlers in the ring. Brick Shithouse grunts. Merlin, for his part, maintains his fearless serial killer stare.

"Uh, Merlin," I yank his drenched sleeve. "Move aside."

I'm going to give Brick Shithouse the benefit of the doubt. He's not trying to pick a fight. The deck is narrow and Merlin was in his way.

As I clear Merlin out of his path, Brick Shithouse nods at me. "Thank you," Brick Shithouse mumble-growls at me.

"You're very welcome," I say.

I like him.

Merlin scowls. "There's something fishy afoot aboard this *Tiger Blood*."

"Yeah, no shit." I whirl on Mordred. "What are you going to do?"

"They have disrespected me," he says, kicking up his feet and biting into the butt end of a Cuban cigar. "I will teach them a lesson."

"Does this lesson involve murder?"

He tosses his head back and laughs, cigar clammed between his teeth. "I am not my mother's son."

I frown. Technically, he *is* Morgaine's son.

"I do not kill for pleasure." He signals his henchmen. "Show them how I feel about littering in my ocean."

"Yes, Boss," Weasel says.

Brick Shithouse nods and hoists his machine gun into the air...

And they open fire, spraying the water with bullets.

"Oh shit!" I dive for cover, shielding my arms over my head. Merlin joins me on the floor. I squeeze my eyes shut, waiting for the gun fire to end. It seems to go on forever. What are these guys doing? Emptying a hundred rounds into my attackers?

At long last... silence.

I summon up the courage to rise, expecting to see a blood-bath: bullet ridden corpses, an ocean drenched with blood.

The Sea-Doo guys are miles away, hauling ass away from *Tiger Blood*. The fisherman is alive and well, sputtering toward shore on a sinking boat.

"See?" Mordred approaches us with two flutes of chilled champagne. "We just scared them a little."

I clear my throat and eye his henchmen. "So where'd'you meet these guys?"

Mordred smiles. "College."

16

MORDRED STEERS his cigarette boat in-land through swampy routes cloaked by waist-high reeds. The brackish water is netted by vegetation, and if one looked closely enough, one could see that the floating log actually has eyes.

Merlin jumps. "What in blazes is that?"

"Gators." I swat a mosquito from my arm.

"Blimey! It's the ugliest thing I've ever seen."

"Somehow I doubt that."

For someone who has been to the Jurassic Era, fought a ptero-dactyl, and tamed a T-Rex, he sure is making a big deal over a little alligator.

The air in the Florida Everglades is as humid as my bathroom after a scorching hot bath. My hair is fizzled. The mosquitos are eating me alive. I'm not the only one who has complaints about the heat and humidity. Merlin, who up until this point, has only known cool British climes, is beginning to resemble an over-watered house plant. Not that I object to the sweat glistening from his stacked chest, but the more he stews in the swamp, the more he yearns for home.

I approach Mordred with all due caution. He's handed over

the steering to Weasel and is sitting back in the cushioned built-in seats, barking orders on his gigantic brick-shaped cell phone.

"If I don't have the money by noon tomorrow, I shall be very upset, my friend." He sounds calm and unruffled. The opposite of Morgaine and her bloody temper. "Noon. Tomorrow."

"What's happening at noon?" I ask as soon as he finishes his call.

"Just a bit of business," he says, tossing his cell phone to Brick Shithouse. "Here you go, Ernest."

I gawk at the hulking henchman. He's got to be pushing seven feet. *Ernest?*

"What kind of business are you in, Mordred?"

A pause. "Shipping."

"Shipping what?"

"I import and export," Mordred clears his throat, "certain items."

"What kind of items?"

"Just things."

"What kind of things?"

He places a hand on my thigh. "This and that."

I narrow my eyes and study Mordred. "Okay."

I'm going to go out on a limb and believe him. Why shouldn't he be a regular ole importer/exporter? Just because his college buddies sprayed my pursuers with bullets, it's not like they killed anybody. For all I know, everyone in Florida is armed like third world dictators. After all, it's Florida.

The boat creeps into a secluded mangrove grove. "Where are we going?"

"We're going to unload some of my cargo and then, I will show you my favorite club in Miami." Mordred takes a handful of my hair and smells it.

I swat his hand away. "Don't get fresh on me, kid. What happens at the club?"

Mordred's dark eyes twinkle. "We dance."

## 17

AFTER DROPPING OFF HIS 'SPECIAL' cargo at a secret swamp warehouse, it's back to Ocean Drive to *The Throne Room*, Mordred's late night hangout.

I've never heard of it, but *The Throne Room* was one of the hottest clubs in the '80s until a fire razed it to its foundations in the mid-'90's. All this I learned from Merlin, who has been browsing Wikipedia while brooding in the backseat of Mordred's pink Cadillac.

South Beach is buzzing with colorful nightlife. The line out the door is a block long.

Brick Shithouse leads us past the lines and peers over his tiny sunglasses at the bouncer who looks like he could be Brick Shithouse's brother.

The bouncer waves us through and we meander across lush purple carpets. We squeeze pass dancers in sequins and spandex doing the most awkward moves (I call them full scale body jerks) on a polished onyx dance floor. There's a wall of mirrors broken by replicas of Greek statues. Our VIP booth is decorated in lush purple velvet flanked by two gigantic urns filled with plum and teal ostrich feathers.

Weasel starts ordering drinks for the table, but declines to sit with us. He guards one side of our booth. Brick Shithouse blocks Mordred from public view, his hostile gaze scanning every corner of the nightclub.

Geez. For an importer/exporter, Mordred certainly seems paranoid.

"Are we expecting trouble?" I ask. "Don't they want to join us?"

Mordred smiles as if my question is silly. "They will stand."

Merlin fidgets in his seat.

"Something the matter, *Uncle*?"

Merlin scowls at Mordred, his dislike for the kid clear. "I would like to visit the water closet," he eyes Brick Shithouse's back, "but someone is in my way."

"That's an easy fix, Uncle Merlin."

"Again," Merlin says, "I'm not your uncle."

Mordred snaps a finger. "Weasel. Escort Merlin to the bathroom."

"Yes, Boss."

"I can find the water closet myself," Merlin says.

"It's a confusing place," Mordred says. "You may get lost. I *insist* that you bring a buddy."

Leaning forward, Merlin rolls up his sleeves and plants his palms on the table.

*Stubborn ass.*

I level him with a look of warning. "Merlin, just take Weasel with you. We can all use a buddy system when we pee."

Merlin opens his mouth to protest, but one growl from Brick Shithouse and he backs down. He gets up reluctantly. Weasel tails him.

Now that we have the VIP booth to ourselves, Mordred sidles up to me, draping an arm around my bare shoulders. "I don't think Uncle Merlin likes me."

"Merlin is grumpy on the outside, total teddy bear on the inside."

"Hm. Much like Ernest."

Brick Shithouse turns at the sound of his name. I give him a little wave. He nods back.

"Do you like your new dress?" Mordred asks, fingering one of my spaghetti straps.

Did I tell you Mordred bought me a club outfit?

It's a slinky silver backless number with matching chandelier earrings and five inch pumps. I'm relieved I don't have to use my magic powers to change our outfits. *Whew.*

Mordred even lent Merlin one of his linen leisure suits. See how nice he is? I don't know why Merlin has it out for Mordred.

"I don't like the way Merlin scowls at me," Mordred says. "Like he wants to pummel my face into putty. Do you not see it, Laurel Kirby?"

"It's because he has beef with your mom," I say. "And he's projecting it onto you."

"I think..." His breath fans my cheeks as he brushes my hair behind my ear. "...he's jealous of *us?*"

"Us?"

Mordred's eyes are a sultry imitation of his mother's. Oh shit. Baby Mordred *is* coming onto me.

My shock dissolves into shaky laughter. I gently nudge his hand from my thigh. "Mordred, I'm old enough to be your mother."

"Not true," he says. "Technically, I was born before you."

"Yeah, but we're not counting decades. We're talking about right here, right now."

He comes dangerously close to nipping my earlobe. "I like older women and I have my eye on you. Come. Let us dance."

Who does this kid think he is? My eyes shift to the side. I wonder if Morgaine is eavesdropping. I've done my best to block her from my mind, but she has a way of sneaking in.

*Morgaine, in case you're watching, I'm not trying to start anything with Mordred. He's coming onto me.*

Mordred tugs me to the end of a conga line. His hands settle on my waist as we snake around the dance floor.

"Hey! Is that Gloria Estefan?" I shout over the music. Despite my reservations, my shoulders shake on their own accord as we dance to the rhythm of the night.

After our third turn, I feel Mordred try to cop a feel again. He's grinding against me, his pelvis gyrating clockwise, then counter-clockwise.

"Yo! What are you doing?" I break from the conga line, hoping to shrug Mordred off, but he latches onto me like a horny tick.

Mordred spins me around and yanks me toward him. His stare is smoldering and serious, and his hips are sending me a direct message. Mordred wants to bone.

I'm not sure how I feel about that. On the one hand, I knew him as a baby. Does that make me his foster aunt? On the other hand, he is a successful small business owner. And he *is* hot. Plus, it would really piss off Morgaine if I got involved with her son. Like astronomically piss her off.

And it's not like I'm getting any action from Merlin. I glance around the nightclub. Where is he anyway? How long does it take him to pee?

Mordred's hands snake up my naked back and his breath is hot against my temple. "Why don't you say we ditch these losers and have a drink at my place?"

I arch an eyebrow. "Wow, you're good."

A smug nod. "Thank you."

"What about Merlin?"

"I'll have my men take him wherever he wants to go."

That probably sounded more ominous than he meant it to be.

I narrow my eyes. "Why don't *you* like Merlin?"

"He does not like *me*. I remember him giving me funny looks when I was a baby. I always got the impression he wanted me dead."

"Wait... you *remember*?"

"Yeah."

Wow. He must have been one attentive baby.

"Merlin doesn't want you dead." *He isn't exactly happy that you're alive.* "He's just concerned about the king and the throne."

"You know what else I remember?" Mordred leans in and peeks down at my cleavage. "You holding me next to that sweet, sweet rack."

Dude. Mordred is just asking for a sexual harassment lawsuit. "I helped change your diaper too. And you peed on me. All over my face."

"I know," his voice slides into a seductive growl, "and I would like to again..."

Um... Okay. *What?!!!*

I pry his hands off me. "Look Mordred, I don't know what kind of kinky shit you're into, but count me out. If you think—"

"What are they doing?" Mordred glances past my shoulder.

Merlin, accompanied by Weasel, is coming toward us.

To my left, Brick Shithouse is rushing for us, but he gets sidelined by another conga line.

A man in a powder blue linen suit makes a beeline toward us. He's tall and broad shouldered and sporting a full-on crunchy mullet. That is, way more nasty than Mordred's half-mullet.

The mullet man reaches us first. "Are you Mordred?"

Mordred cocks an eyebrow. "I am..."

"Santino sends his greetings."

Mordred's eyes widen. He pushes me back and reaches inside his coat.

The man bellows, "Yah!" and jumps into the air. He's about to roundhouse kick Mordred in the face when, out of the blue, a hand catches the man's ankle mid-kick. Disco light glints off the switch blade hidden in the toe of the assassin's boot.

Mordred and I back away, our gazes following the deadly boot to the person holding the ankle.

"Merlin!"

Merlin winks at me. And with a similar "Yah!" he slams his elbow down on the assassin's shin. SNAP. The leg is toast.

In seconds, Brick Shithouse pushes past the conga line and has the howling assassin in a chokehold. CRACK. The assassin drops to the floor.

The assassination attempt plunges the nightclub into chaos.

Aimed screams and a fifty-person stampede toward the exit, someone fires a gun.

The mirror behind us shatters.

It's every man for himself.

"Find cover!" Mordred shouts at us. He's got two pistols in his hands, Brick Shithouse at his back, and Weasel canvassing the club with an Uzi.

Where were they hiding these guns? Guess that's the perk of oversized blazers and baggy trousers.

Dark shadows zoom in the corners. Someone fires at Mordred from the bar, misses.

Brick Shithouse unleashes a rain of bullets... *bratatat bratatat ratatatat ratatatat*

Oh man!

Merlin and I dive beneath a table. It's a nightclub fire fight and we don't want to be caught in the crossfire.

"Santino! You fuck!" Mordred shouts. "I've got your number!"

*bratatat... bratatat ratatatat ratatatat*

It sounds like he somehow got his hands on a machine gun.

I shield my head. "What is going on here? Who is Santino and what does he want with Mordred? And what's with the guy with the knife boot?"

"Santino is the *second* biggest drug smuggler and gun runner in Miami," Merlin says. "Can you guess who's the first?"

I squeeze my eyes shut. "I thought Baby Mordred was an importer/exporter!"

"He is! He imports and exports drugs."

*Holy shit!* "Who told you this?"

"Nestor."

"Nestor?" I frown. "You mean *Weasel*? Do you talk while you pee?"

"Aye," Merlin says. "One can glean much information at this 'urinal.'"

We both jump as a body crashes on our table. I poke my head out. Jesus Christ! It's a blood bath! Dead bodies everywhere. The bar is shot to shit. Mirrored walls—shattered.

Weasel, I mean, Nestor has been gut shot. Mordred is on top of the bar, machine gunning down a cluster of men and cursing Santino's mother.

"Morgaine isn't kidding. Mordred really did get mixed up with a bad crowd." I jump again when a heavy body hits the floor beside us.

Noooooooooooooooooo! Brick Shithouse. He never hurt a soul!

Mordred is holding down the fort against an army.

"We need to get him out!"

"He can hold his own," Merlin says.

"Morgaine is going to be super pissed if we let Mordred die. Come on, Merlin. We have to help him."

Merlin grumbles. "We are not armed."

"Oh, we're armed." I flex my sorceress hands. "Ready?"

Merlin rolls his eyes. "Do you have a plan?"

"Don't get shot!" I rush into the fray, sorceress hands blazing.

18

---

I DON'T KNOW how I get into these situations. All I ever wanted was peace and quiet—and to reach 1 million Instagram followers. Simple goals. What do I get instead? A bunch of '80s goons in bad polyester suits shooting at me. Weasel is dead. Brick Shithouse is dead.

Mordred takes a bullet to the knee and goes down.

*Mordred! Noooooo!*

I pop out of my hiding place just as Mordred kills the guy who shot him and rolls behind the bar for cover. He hears my cry and gives me a cheerful thumbs up.

I'm super pissed. My hands are locked and loaded with magic. I fully intend to whoop ass with my new powers.

Behind me, a section of wall crumbles from a hail of bullets. The shooter reloads his Uzi, a cigar clenched between his teeth.

"Oh my God. What an asshole!" I raise my arms and summon up earth, wind, and fire (and *heart* because you can't whoop ass without heart). Pink lightning collects at my fingertips and I'm just about to hurl it at the shooter when he takes a blue blast to the chest and crashes into a faux Roman column, stunned but (fingers crossed) not dead.

"You take too long." Merlin pops up behind me. He blows on his smoking fingers.

"I was trying to take him down with heart. I don't want to kill anyone."

"Perhaps you should find cover," Merlin rolls up his sleeves, "your pink powers mark you as weak. Go tend to Mordred and let me clear this strange purple pub."

I'm pretty sure Merlin just mansplained magic to me. Also, I resent him making fun of my pink lightning hands. I didn't choose the color! If it were up to me, I'd have preferred something more gender neutral, like green or yellow. Or badass like black... black lightning would be the—

Whoa!

A second shooter jumps out of the shadows, ready to unload on us.

"Oh no you don't!" I take aim.

ZAP!

An electric pink net sails out of my fingertips and flattens him to the floor. He's cursing and yelling like a maniac. The more he struggles, the more the net tightens and zaps.

"Ow!" My assailant pulls his hand back and spins in a circle on the floor. "It's electrocuting me!"

Talk about melodramatic. I've totally dialed down the intensity of the electric shock (wouldn't want a repeat shark explosion). This new and improved net gives a tiny shock like the kind hamsters get during lab experiments, which is cruel for hamster but just what this asshole deserves.

"Maybe you should have thought of that before you entered a life of gun violence!"

With a nod at Merlin, we canvass the nightclub. My electric net proves the most effective (and bloodless) solution. After coordinating with Merlin's blue lightning, all of Santino's mercenaries are flopping around in nets like an unsavory catch of tuna.

I grab Mordred's gigantic cell phone and alert the police.

"That was brilliant! Both of you." Mordred says as I tear up a table cloth and wrap it around his leg wound. "If you ever need a job, I have an opening on my team — "

"Pipe down, asshole. I've had enough out of you."

"Me? I'm an asshole?"

"You got Brick Shithouse killed, and I was just beginning to like him."

With a blink, Mordred gazes around the corpse-littered dance floor. He swallows a lump in his throat and crawls toward Brick Shithouse's lifeless bulk. Mordred hangs his head. "Ernest... he was a good man. Never harmed a soul."

"Um... he mowed down that group of bodies by the bar. Weasel's dead too."

"Not Nestor!"

Mordred crawls toward Weasel's corpse and closes the dead man's eyes. He shakes a fist over Weasel's body. "I'm going to take it out of their skulls."

"Whose skulls?" I whisper.

"Santino's," Mordred says.

"Why didn't you just say 'his' skull?"

"I'm trying to have a moment here!" Mordred snaps.

Geez. Melodramatic *and* an explosive temper... just like his mother.

"Unless you want to have your moment in the backseat of a police car, come with me." Tightening his tourniquet, I drag him up by the elbow. He drapes an arm over Merlin's shoulders and we haul him out of the club.

Twenty minutes later, we dump Mordred on the carpet of Morgaine and Vicky's suite at the hotel.

I slap my hands together. "Here's your asshole son. Safe and sound."

"He's wounded," Morgaine frowns.

"He took a bullet to the knee."

Mordred raises himself on his elbow. "You should have seen

the other guys."

I narrow my eyes at Mordred. "He killed *so* many people."

"I didn't kill anyone who wasn't trying to kill me first."

Morgaine folds her arms across her chest. She's wearing a black satin lingerie set and it looks like she's just finished her night routine. Her lotion smells like shea butter and coconut.

Vicky stands beside her with her face in a cucumber clay mask, an oversized Miami Dolphins jersey, and teeny tiny shorts.

"Mother." Mordred's gaze travels up Vicky's bare leg. "Who's the babe?"

Vicky props her hands on her hips. She looks like she's on the verge of planting her foot in his face. *"Babe?"*

"Have a little respect for your future stepmother," I say, glancing over my shoulder.

Merlin is helping himself to Morgaine and Vicky's half-finished chocolate fondue.

Fondue!

Great. While I was being chased down by drunks in Sea-Doos and shot at by the Miami cartels, Morgaine and Vicky are living it up in a penthouse suite and feasting on chocolate dipped straw-berries. After the day I had, I could use some chocolate!

"Save some for me, Merlin!"

A thumbs up.

Morgaine frowns as she looks over her son's bullet wound. I hope she doesn't blame me for Mordred getting shot. He got himself shot. She's muttering something to him and I can tell by his hung head and shrinking shoulders that he's getting a dressing down. Maybe he's grounded, the little shit.

I clear my throat. "Morgaine, a word with you?" I cock my head toward door. "In private?"

She nods and points at Mordred. "You stay right here and think about what you've done."

"Hey Uncle Merlin," Mordred calls, "can I have a chocolate covered marshmallow?"

"No!" Morgaine says. "Don't give him any food."

"I don't plan to," Merlin says with his mouth full.

She joins me in the hallway. Before she has a chance to thank me (given how I almost got shot up by machine guns, she'd better thank me!), I get down to business. "Okay. Mission accomplished. I've brought Mordred back, who, in addition to being an asshole and a chauvinistic pig, is also a sick sick sicko."

Morgaine's mouth presses into a thin line. "He needs tough love."

"He's been hitting on me all day! Did you know he tried to grab my ass?"

"He does that." Morgaine shakes her head. "Gets it from his good-for-nothing father."

"Yeah, well, when you said he got mixed up with the wrong crowd, you should have told me I was dealing with freakin' Scarface! Anyway. No matter. He's back. Bargain fulfilled. Now hand over my soul."

She responds to my every word with a solemn nod. At long last, she holds up her hands. The Rubik's Cube containing 1/7th of my soul materializes in her fingers like a poison apple. "Here you go."

Wow. That was easy. I expected Morgaine to break her word and make me fight her for the Rubik's Cube. "That's it? You're not going to drag your heels over this?"

She shrugs. "A deal's a deal."

I take the Rubik's Cube from her, expecting it to burn my hands. Other than the purple neon glow, it feels ordinary and surprisingly light. Does that mean my soul is lean and lacking of substance?

Nah. I *totally* have substance.

"So when does the soul swap happen?"

"When you solve the cube."

"That's all?" Need I remind her that I solved the Rubik's Cube in three seconds flat? I sure as hell can do it again. Maybe I'll set a new world record.

"That's all," Morgaine says.

"Can I keep the powers?"

"Yes," Morgaine says.

"Really?"

"Until you solve the cube."

Damn. I see what she did there. It's up to me. I'll remain a badass sorceress as long as I procrastinate.

"What about Operation Royal Takeover?" I arch my eyebrow. "Bet you're itching to suck me into your throne usurping plans."

Morgaine throws her hands up in the air. "I have my hands full with Mordred." She sighs. "And Vicky. She is quite demanding too."

"Hence the chocolate fondue." I nod in understanding. It's hard to be a single mother and a tender lesbian lover while plotting world domination. I have to admire Morgaine. Some women really deserve their shoulder pads.

"So where does this leave us?" I ask. "Are we not doing Operation Royal Takeover?"

"We'll get to it."

"When?"

Morgaine does a palms up. "You have the Rubik's Cube and MorgVPN. This isn't your first rodeo through time. Start without me."

"But—"

"Seriously, Laurel! Do I have to hold your hand every time?"

She leaves me to attend to her son.

Well! This wasn't the Morgaine le Fey I was expecting. The Morgaine I know would've fought me tooth and nail for possession of my soul. This Morgaine acts like she doesn't even want it, and frankly, I'm a little offended. She's treating my soul like it's the leftover item on a holiday discount shelf. I don't care about her apathy. She's acting like... like *me*. Why didn't anyone tell me I was so annoying?!

I turn the Rubik's Cube over in my hands. I can solve it now and put an end to our soul pact.

Or...

I can join the group in the penthouse suite for chocolate fondue and then party all night long with my sorceress powers while I still have them. Choices choices...

With a shrug, I pocket the Rubik's Cube and enter the suite. Why do stuff today what you can procrastinate until tomorrow?

19

---



"WHAT DO you mean you're leaving tomorrow?!"

I nearly choke on my room service cheeseburger. After a *long* day, I've finally kicked my feet up, slapped on a rejuvenating clay mask, and channel surfed through the hotel's four channels. You can't really Netflix & Chill in 1987. They don't know what Netflix is. But I do have the *Golden Girls* on at 9 pm and oh look! *Who's the Boss.*

Merlin and I are in our hotel room. It's smaller and less bougie than Morgaine's penthouse, but we have a jacuzzi, a 26" television, and a king-size bed shaped like a clamshell. The furniture reminds me of Auntie June's house prior to their third renovation: wicker chairs and a beachy coral/aquamarine color palette. I have my cheeseburger and fries, chocolate milkshake and margarita nightcap (on Morgaine's tab) and was all ready to relax.

Until Merlin rained on my parade.

"When tomorrow?" I gasp, unable to believe my ears.

"Noon."

*That's so soon!*

"I've made plans for a group outing to Disney World! If you

think theme park day in California is fun, wait till we visit Disney World!" I pout. "Can't you delay your plans for a day?"

"No."

"Not at all?"

"Such is the way of wizards."

What the fuck is that even suppose too mean? "It doesn't have to be."

"Alas, it is."

Gah! I can't reason with this fool! Merlin mentioned going back to his time, but I thought he was over it. We were having so much fun in the '80s. Or if he was serious, I assumed he wouldn't be ready until at least the end of the week.

"Our mission is complete. Mordred is returned. My time has ended." Merlin shakes his head. "I shall miss you, Laurel Kirby. You will forever have a place in my — " He pounds a soulful fist to his rock-hard chest.

Yeah. Yeah. I get it. That's about as emotional as Merlin gets. I wish he'd stop telling me how much he'll miss me. He doesn't have to miss me if he chooses to stay. What does Arthur need him for? I'm sure he can find another wizard advisor to replace Merlin. Isn't the Dark Ages full of them?

"What if you return at 12:30?"

"No."

I arch an eyebrow. "12:01?"

He makes excuses about the winter solstice, the earth aligning with the sun, which in turns aligns with the moon. Whatever. All I know is that by noon tomorrow I will be minus one wizard friend.

The Rubik's Cube burns like a lump of hot coal in my purse. I should note that I'm not *wearing* my purse in the hotel room. Duh, it's chilling on the coat rack, but I can sense it burning and pulsing like the demonic Rubik's Cube it is.

Should I tell Merlin about my soul pact/power swap with

Morgaine? If he knew about the cosmic shit show we're dealing with *here*, in 1987, he couldn't go back!

Okay.

I'm totally going to tell him. And even though I have the power to solve the Rubik's Cube and end my creepy soul connection with Morgaine...

I won't do it. Not yet. I'll do it, eventually. After Disney World. Maybe I can solve the Cube but *pretend* Morgaine and I are still connected. Think Merlin will buy it?

My stomach is heavy with shame and greasy cheeseburgers and I think I have gas. See where mingling your soul with an evil sorceress' soul will lead you? Manipulation! Duplicity! Lies! I can't even *believe* I'm thinking about maintaining my freak connection with Morgaine. First thing tomorrow, I'm going to solve the fuck out of that Rubik's Cube and end it.

Then I'll say goodbye to Merlin forever.

I sigh. "I'll miss you too, Merlin."

He helps himself to my fries. "What will you like to do on our last night together? Shall we eat more of this chocolate fountain?"

"I suppose there's a buffet we can check out. They serve lobster."

"Lobster!" His eyes light up. "What are we waiting for?"

Defeated, I leave my dinner and sit down on the edge of the clam shell bed. The mattress wobbles beneath me. I flop on my back. The sensation is like bobbing in a pool. "Holy Shit, Merlin! Hop on here! It's a waterbed!"

"What is a waterbed?"

"A bed made of water instead of straw."

Merlin gives me a skeptical look. He's still getting used to the concept of box springs so you can imagine how revolutionary a waterbed is to his Medieval mind.

Merlin body surfs onto the mattress and nearly bounces me to the floor. Pure joy lights his sexy face. "I have seen many things,

Laurel Kirby, but I have never beheld a bed made of water. What matter of people have fashioned this?"

"Kinky people, that's who."

As Merlin settles in the middle of our waterbed, his shirt rides up, revealing a scrumptious amount of rock hard abs. The sight of his skin heats up my body. Mmm. Break me off a piece of *that*.

I've been objectifying Merlin since he rescued me on horseback. He was wearing tight buckskin breeches and a variety of leather goods. Images of Merlin in all his sexy costume changes flickers through my mind:

Merlin in blue velvet robes with the belt casually... undone.

Merlin in Regency England... when he was the hottest vicar in the village.

And now Merlin in his Miami Vice blazer with the sleeves rolled up, naked ankles above his loafers. Okay. I didn't know this until today: I have a fetish for naked ankles.

Considering all my pent up lust for Merlin, I've never made a move... Not a real move outside of fake kissing at Vicky's wedding rehearsal and that kiss had sizzled every nerve ending in my body.

I sit up (Or try to. Waterbeds really suck you in, don't they?) as a brilliant new idea pops into my head.

Why hadn't it occurred to me before?

I don't need sorcery or soul pacts to convince Merlin to stay.

Am I an influencer or am I an influencer?

If I choose, I can elicit quite a *seductive* influence...

Tonight, with the Miami moonlight streaming through our window, a jacuzzi, a waterbed, and chocolate-covered strawberries, Merlin is never going to want to leave my side.

Tonight...

We are going to fuck.

## 20

DID I SAY 'FUCK'?

I might have been overzealous in my sex plans. I pulled my groin at the nightclub and fucking sounds like a lot of cardio, and Lord knows I don't need that.

So I was thinking, a slow candlelit lovemaking: Rose petals on the bed. Sensual R&B. Merlin does all the work. *That's* what we're going for.

Except one problem: Merlin is more interested in channel surfing than in boning me.

Merlin hasn't moved from the foot of the bed all night. He's been flipping through the same four channels, pausing intermittently on the news. I might as well be invisible.

I've emerged from the jacuzzi, which I soaked in, alone.

I'm toweling my hair and I've lotion up every inch of my body with the hotel's gardenia-scented lotion, which smells incredible but isn't exactly gentle on sensitive skin.

After trying on a number of lingerie combos in the bathroom (wardrobe change with the snap of a finger), I settled on a soft terry cloth bathrobe with nothing on underneath. Merlin doesn't appreciate my outfits on a normal day. Something tells me that cute lingerie would go right over his head. He'll never take interest unless I'm covered in mashed potatoes and a sirloin steak.

Naked it shall be.

Let the seduction begin.

Channeling Cleopatra, I drape myself across the waterbed, arms over my head, bare legs exposed. I've loosen the belt on my bathrobe, displaying peekaboo cleavage.

"Merlin?" I say to his turned back.

"Huh?"

"Would you like a chocolate-covered strawberry?"

"In a minute." He pauses on a baseball game.

"A sip of champagne?"

He tilts his head as the pitcher tosses a curveball.

"Merlin?" I bounce the waterbed, sending a wave undulating toward him. I'm not sure about this waterbed. It's making me sea sick. "Come talk to me. I'm lonely..."

He reaches behind him and taps my foot. "Maybe you should sit in that chair and tend to your Instagram."

*What the—*

"Yo Merlin!"

"Huh?"

Enough is enough! Crawling toward him, I snatch the remote from his hands, turn off the TV, and toss the remote across the room.

"Hey!" Merlin finally whirls around.

I smack him on the shoulder. "This is our last night together and you'd rather watch TV."

"There's no TV where I'm from..." He finally looks at me.

Between the crawling and the bouncing waterbed, my robe seemed to have parted. "You're naked!"

"That's right." With a shy smile, I let my robe slip from my shoulders and pool around my waist. "It's our last night together. I've decided to give you something to remember me by."

"You want to make the beast with two backs?"

I frown. Not exactly the most romantic image, but I'll take it. "I think it's time we take this relationship to the next level."

Merlin never blushes. He's red as a tomato now. His serial killer eyes smolders as his gaze passes over my breast, down my navel, and settles on my...

He jumps up, shocked and scandalized, but also, judging by the impressive trouser tent he's sporting... *up* for anything. "Laurel Kirby! What did you do to yourself?!"

"What?" I glance down at all the fuss. "Oh, that. It's called a Brazilian. Very necessary for high cut bikinis."

"It's ah..." Merlin tugs on his collar. "I've never seen anything so... bare."

I suppose women in the Dark Ages didn't have the time or the tools to trim their hedges. Imagine trying to landscape down there with those rustic scissors I used to give King Arthur and his Knights their haircuts. Ouch. That being said, I imagine women of his time kept things au naturel.

Leveling him with my most sultry gaze, I discard my robe and scoot toward him.

I take a deep breath. Okay. Moment of truth.

I open my legs a little and have the pleasure of watching his jaw drop and his body go rigid.

A moment of silence. I know. *I know.* You prudes out there must think I'm a brazen *hussy*:

Having my goods on display...

Hoping Merlin will treat my body like an All-You-Can-Eat buffet...

I dearly hope there will be a lot of eating involved, so it's my duty, as a woman who knows what her vagina likes, to steer his face...into it.

"Would you like to take a closer look?"

Merlin clears his throat. "I would like to inspect your wares," he says in a strangled voice.

I hide my smile. "Do you have to do it with your clothes on?"

He tugs his shirt over his head, briefly sending me into six pack heaven before he jumps me and we make waves on the waterbed.

21

THE THING about sex in a clamshell-shaped water bed is...

Meh.

It's not the most comfortable. You're slipping and sliding and you can't really angle right. I've never tried to bone on a life raft, but I suspect that's how it feels like.

Merlin may be a 10 in the bod department, an 9.5 in the brain department, but guys... he's a 4.5 in the sack.

He sucks.

*HE SUCKS!*

In his defense, he came from the Arthurian Age and if you've stuck around this far, that's like *darker* than the Dark Age and one step above cavemen sex. I don't think he gets the concept of foreplay. In fact, I don't think foreplay was even invented. The priests gathered up all the men of the land and told them the story of Adam & Eve, the gist of which is to say 'Fuck Eve' she doesn't deserve an orgasm.

Well, screw that. I plan to orgasm because... feminism.

"Ouch!" I swat Merlin on the shoulders.

He pokes his head up. "What's wrong?"

"Stop it."

"I'm only doing what you told me to do."

I prop myself up on my elbows. I know the first time you have sex with someone is awkward. They don't know what you like. You have to tell them what you like, which may be difficult to voice depending on how comfortable you are with your body and your relationship status.

Fortunately for me, I have no problem criticizing Merlin. I've been doing it since the moment we've met. I guess that's the level of intimacy that comes with sleeping with your friends. You get to tell them:

"You're tending to the wrong area!"

Merlin kisses my inner thigh. "Your 'area' is very complicated. I did not realize there's so much going on down there. Let me show you what *the* Merlin is good at."

With a crooked grin, he covers me with his body and settles himself between my legs.

"Do you like this?" He swirls his hips around, causing the waterbed to bounce and undulate.

"Not bad," I say, "Try counterclockwise wise."

He does, working his darnedest to make me feel good and eventually, after the third rotation, I arch my back and moan like a cat who's been rubbed in just the right places.

He bites my chin. "Does Laurel Kirby like?"

"Oh, Laurel likes... I like. Don't stop."

He arches an eyebrow, sounding mighty proud of himself. "It is time."

"Time for what?"

"My staff must seek its sheath."

My eyes snap open. "Okay, first off. Don't *ever* use that analogy again. Second, what's the rush? You've got a train to catch?"

Merlin melts me into the mattress with his sexy sinister stare. "I enjoy it when you treat me like the serfs."

And I feel that he is, indeed, enjoying my brand of dirty talk. So Merlin wants to be subjugated and made low like he's on the bottom rung of the feudal system, eh? Sicko. We can make that happen.

"All right, you damn dirty peasant. Make sure you're now leaving my fields uh... fallow."

That gets his engines running and I wholeheartedly approve of what he's doing to my body. He's paying homage to my breast, massaging up my naughty bits, prepping it for... plowing.

The waterbed bobs up and down. I shut my eyes, luxuriating in the hot wizard and his hotter kisses when I start to feel disconnected.

Like I'm having an out-of-body experience.

Except I don't *want* to have an out-of-body experience.

I want to be *in* my body before Merlin gets *in* me. I'm floating above the bed with a great view of Merlin's *fine* ass. As pleasing as that sight is, I wonder why I'm not under him instead of hovering over him like a ghost in *A Christmas Carol*.

Suddenly a neon purple light blinds me and I get the feeling that I'm not alone. I check over my shoulder. I'm not the only ghost in the room. Morgaine freaking le Fey is floating beside me, checking out Merlin's ass too.

"What the fuck is going on here?!"

Morgaine strokes her chin and watches the show. "Looks like you're having more fun than I am at the moment. Let's swap, shall we?"

"Swap?" What is she talking about? "Get out of my room!"

Imagine! Peeping in on my most intimate moment. I've never heard of such depravity. I raise a feeble ghost hand. I'm going to smack the shit out of her!

Before I can let her have it, I'm blinded by a flash of purple light and the next thing I know, I'm being sucked into a tunnel.

I flail my arms, hollering and cursing at the top of my lungs as I fly through a star field. Synthpop blasts in my ears and vectors of neon upside down triangles assault me from all sides. It's the sky vortex all over again, except 'make it '80s.'

I glance down. The ground is covered in neon grid lines. Where the fuck am I? Am I in the Rubik's Cube?!

"Morgaine!" I land with a thump in a plush arm chair and immediately gasp for air.

"What's wrong with you, Morgaine?" It's Vicky. She's pacing in front of me and sounding mad as hell. "Have you been listening to a word I've said?"

I glance down at lap. I'm *not* naked. I'm dressed in a purple spandex one piece with scrunchie socks pulled up to my ankles.

*What the hell?*

My eyes dart to the foot of the bed. Mordred lounges on his side, his leg wrapped up in linen bandages. He's aggressively flipping channels. Where's the clam shell water bed? Where's naked Hot Merlin?

"Of course she's not listening," Mordred shoots me a resentful side-eye, "she never listens."

I shake my head. "What are you guys doing in my room?"

"What are you talking about?" Vicky props her hands on her hips. "This is *our* room. Don't you even *think* about playing dumb. We've gotta do something about your punk kid!"

"I'm not a kid," Mordred says, without taking his eyes off the television. "I'm more man than you can handle, Legs."

"Shut up, you little shit."

"If I'm a shit," Mordred says, "it's *her* fault."

I massage my temples. "*My* fault?"

"Yes." Mordred rolls his eyes. "See? Not listening again."

"What about Morgaine?" I say.

Vicky's nostrils flare. "I don't know what mind games you're playing at, Morgaine, but it's not working."

*"Why are you calling me Morgaine?! I'm Laurel."*

"Oh no you don't! Don't bring Laurel into this."

"What about—"

Mordred chucks his remote on the mattress and jams an angry finger at me. "What about *you*, Mom? *What about you*?"

Vicky whirls on me. "Morgaine! Are you hearing this? Morgaine?"

Morgaine? Mom? Why are they calling me...

I stumble to the gauzy walled mirror behind the bed. The face staring back at me isn't my own. I touch my sculpted cheekbones and bat my smoky eyes.

Holy shit. I'm Morgaine! I'm in her body.

Wait. If I'm in her body, that means...

"Fuccccccccccckkkkkkkkkkkkkkkkkkk!"

## 22

I'M inside Morgaine's body.

Morgaine is inside my body.

And right now, after finally figuring out foreplay, Merlin's inside me too.

Only problem is: why am *I* not inside me?

This is the Freaky Friday body swap from hell.

Morgaine has chosen the *absolute worst* time to do a body swap because now Merlin's boning *her*! After all my hard work, she's stolen my just reward.

Let me illustrate how fucked up this is:

I've left my car idling by, patiently waiting for the soccer mom to usher her two kids and their kids' friends into her SUV. Minutes tick by. She's taking her time, buckling in babies, checking her mascara in the rearview mirror, checking Facebook, taking *forever*...

Finally, *finally*... soccer mom backs out. My parking spot is cleared. I'm just about to pull forward when Morgaine swoops in and steals my spot. Did she wait an eternity for that spot? No!

I clutch my... *Morgaine's* hair. "I'm going to kill her!"

Vicky and Mordred share a perplexed look. "*Who* are you going to kill?"

"That sneaky bitch Morgaine!"

Vicky places a hand on my shoulder. "Look, Morg. I know you feel horrible about your shitty parenting, but that's no reason to kill yourself. Repeat after me: you are enough."

Gah! I throw my hands up in the air. "I can't expect you to understand!" I glance down at my outfit. "Why am I dressed like Olivia Newton John?"

"You were about to head down to the gym and do night aerobics," Vicky says. "And here I ask you: is this the best time to do aerobics? Your cardio can wait. Your son has a freakin' bullet in his leg. Shouldn't you do whatever it is you do and try to remove that bullet? Look at the little shit!" She gestures to Mordred. "He's in pain."

Mordred waves at his bandages. "I'm in pain, Mother!"

"Look, Mordred, I don't have time to remove your bullet. You *deserve* that bullet. I hope you lose your leg."

"Morgaine!" Vicky says.

Mordred flops down on his impressive stack of pillows. "See what I'm dealing with here?"

I grit my teeth. So Morgaine swoops into my body and has sex with Merlin and what do I get? Vicky nagging at me. Mordred giving me major attitude. This ugly aerobics outfit. I hate purple! And what are these? Yellow socks?

Why can't she drop me in her body while she's doing something cool? Like power steering her pterodactyl Pepper or bending the universe to her will?

Why can't—

"Argggggh!" I clutch my head and stumble a few paces until my shoulder connects with a wall. I'm hit with that same feeling of disorientation.

"What's wrong, Morgaine?" Vicky asks. "Migraine?"

"She's faking it," Mordred says. "She's always faking a

headache when you want to talk to her about something important."

I knock over a vase and WHOOSH —

I'm sucked back into the neon purple vacuum and swimming with rad vectors. "Ahhhhhhhh!"

BAM.

I'm lying flat on my back in the clamshell bed. Merlin's beside me, a stupid grin on his face. His chest is all sweaty and he looks like he's in need of a good cigarette (except we don't smoke here).

I glance down at my body. Gross. I feel like I've just emerged from of an intense session of hot yoga, exhausted but relaxed — all the tension gone from my shoulders. I also feel strangely sore and stretched out like I usually do when I assume the downward dog pose for too long.

"Laurel Kirby!" Merlin pecks me on the lips. "That was incredible. Who knew you were capable of that!"

Capable of what?! What did I do?

"Uh, Merlin?" I ask. "Can we do that again?"

He props himself up on his elbow. "Greedy little minx. Are you trying to kill *the* Merlin? I'll need a week to recover after that."

Something wet touches my bare ass. I jolt up. "Oh. My. God. Don't tell me you..."

"No, no." Merlin snickers. "That's just the waterbed. It sprung a leak after you suggested I take my..."

The rest of that sentence had to be censored. Oh. My. Freaking. God. I would never suggest that! Morgaine is a super freak.

My eyes widen. I'm rendered speechless.

"Aye. I am surprised you'd want to," Merlin props his arms under his head. "I did not think anything would fit there, but you proved me wrong."

With a yelp, I jump from the bed and grab the Rubik's Cube. This has gone on long enough. It was already invasive enough that Morgaine planted her freaky sorceress spyware inside my mind, but now she's gone too far.

"What are you doing?" Merlin asks, watching me twist the Rubik's Cube this way and that.

"I'm ending things once and for all."

Merlin yawns. "You are very strange, Laurel Kirby."

I furrow my brow. Funny. This is the same method I used to solve the puzzle the first time. It had been so easy, so what's with the technical difficulties?

Perspiration beads my brow as I twist and curse, trying one method after the next. What's wrong with me? Why is this Rubik's Cube impossible to solve when I've already solved it in record time?

After multiple attempts, I slam the Rubik's Cube on the dresser, resigned to the fact that this puzzle is rigged.

Why am I not surprised?

Morgaine le Fey is the queen of rigged games.

"Wake up, you," I tap Merlin on the cheek, "we've got a huge problem."

Merlin yawns. "What is the problem?"

I take a deep breath. "Okay, before I tell you, know that I did this with good intentions..."

I tell him about meeting Morgaine in the airplane bathroom and our soul swap. I hand him the Rubik's Cube and watch him shake his head. Not so much in anger, but worse... disappointment.

"But if I didn't lie with you..." Merlin's scowl deepens and his complexion pales. "Who the bloody hell did I bed?!"

I rub a hand over my face. "You know who."

"Le Fey?!" he squeaks. "I made the beast with two backs with Morgaine Damn Her Eyes Le Fey?!!!"

## 23

---



"MORGAINE! WHERE THE FUCK ARE YOU?"

I stalk through the hotel hallways, my hands charged with murderous pink lightning. Behind me, Merlin and Vicky and Mordred (oh yes, Mordred is with us, after I magically yanked the bullet out of his leg and healed his wound because his negligent and selfish mother is too busy screwing my wizard companion *in my body* and won't lift a finger to help him) form my mob.

Having been chased by bloodthirsty mobs on both of my time traveling adventures, now I finally know what it's like to be in one. I enjoy the strength in numbers and there's nothing like a joint hatred of one person to bring about group bonding.

"Le Fey!" Merlin looks like he'd like nothing better than to go Medieval on Morgaine for violating him. "Come out at once, you rank and wicked witch! I will have satisfaction."

I can't help rolling my eyes. Hasn't she satisfied him enough? By now I'm accustomed to Merlin's slip into Ye Ole English and know he's out to defend his honor. Maybe he intends to challenge her to a wizard's duel.

"Morgaine!" Vicky scans the empty halls. "Just wait until I get my hands on you! *I know what you did!*"

If I'm mad, Vicky is raging, especially after I gave her the lowdown on our soul pact/body swap. While she's not happy about any of it, Morgaine sleeping with Merlin *really* got her goat. I want answers from Morgaine. Vicky is out for blood.

"We're looking in the wrong place," Mordred says, causing us to turn around. "My mother never hides."

I tap my foot. "Where is she?"

Mordred's lips curl into a self-assured grin. "In plain sight. May I?" he gestures down the hall.

He leads us to the hotel gym and sure enough, Morgaine is working on her reps.

She smiles at our arrival, but does not stop pumping iron. "Ah! You all made it. Good. Vicky? Spot me?"

Vicky steps forward, ready to maim, but I push her back. Morgaine is *my* nemesis. This is *my* battle.

"Cut the crap, Morgaine," I say. "You have a lot of explaining to do."

With a smug twist of her lips, Morgaine towels her forehead and switches from weights to single-leg squats. "Such as?"

*Such as? Such as?!*

"Don't play dumb with me. You stole my body and sexually assaulted Merlin."

"You took advantage of me," Merlin says, his face flushed.

"And cheated on me!" Vicky joins in.

Mordred crosses his arms over his chest. "And left me to bleed to death...again."

The three of us turn to him. Wow. Poor Mordred. Is it a wonder Mordred turned to a life of crime with a mother like Morgaine?

"I did NOT give you permission to jump into my body," I say. "That was not part of the plan."

"It was a blip," she says with a grunt. She straightens up and works on the other leg.

I snort. "Meaning you didn't plan it?"

"An accidental side effect of our pact."

"That's bullshit, Morgaine. You floated right by me, checked out Merlin's ass, said 'Looks good. Let's swap.'"

Mordred covers his ears. "Too much information!"

"Sorry," I whisper.

Vicky lunges at Morgaine, but Mordred and I hold her back. "I knew it! I saw you check out Merlin's ass at the mall. You weren't really admiring his pants, were you?"

Morgaine's knees hit the mat. "Won't happen again. I didn't particularly enjoy being in Laurel's body."

"Is that supposed to be an apology?" Vicky asks.

"Yes," Morgaine says matter-of-factly.

Vicky and I throw up our hands in disgust. "Unbelievable," we say in unison.

"Not only have you refused to apologize," Vicky says.

"But you've insulted me," I say. "And speaking of which," I hold up the cursed Rubik's Cube, "I can't solve this."

"Oh Laurel," Morgaine gives me a patronizing smile, "it's not my problem puzzles go over your head."

"You and I both know I solved it before," I say. "You hexed it so I can't solve it again."

Morgaine has ditched the squats and is jogging in place. "Why would I do such a silly thing like that?"

"So you can pop in and out of my body whenever you want! It's not happening, Morgaine."

The more I speak, the more I'm kicking myself for entering into this agreement with Morgaine.

As with all my mistakes, it seemed like a good idea at the time. I give Merlin a reason to stay and I get cool sorceress powers in the mix. In return, Morgaine gets 1/7th of my soul as a retainer. 1/7th of my soul isn't so horrible. I've lost more than that to Instagram.

Now I see the error of my ways. In putting my soul in a

Rubik's Cube, I've given Morgaine a back door into my mind and body. And she's already proven she can't be trusted.

Damn.

When will I ever learn? You'd think the many times she's tried to kill me would've knocked some sense into me.

I shove the Rubik's Cube under Morgaine's nose. "Unhex this."

"Laurel," she shakes her head. "Don't be ridiculous. I would never betray—"

I arch an eyebrow.

Morgaine clears her throat. "I never betrayed you *this time*."

"A bald-faced lie if I ever heard one."

"Look," she says, slowly backing away to the corner of the floor mat, "there's an aerobics class starting in a few minutes. Why don't all you join me?"

"Morgaine! Unhex the Cube!"

"You have my powers, Laurel. Surely you can solve a simple little puzzle. In the meantime, aerobics class?"

"What's with your obsession with aerobics?" Vicky says. "We're talking about Laurel's *soul* here and all you care about is burning body fat."

"Yeah, Morgaine," I say. "Nobody is interested in aerobics."

"A shame," Morgaine stretches her arm over her head, "because look what I learned to do..."

Before I can retort, she backflips on the mat like a gymnast, and even in my skepticism, I have to admit that she's got good form. She leads with a straight jump, then moves into a switch leap followed by a cartwheel.

"Now you're just showing off," I say.

"She likes attention," Mordred says.

"She did that in bed," Merlin mutters when Morgaine does the splits. "I rather enjoyed it."

"Shut up, Merlin," I snap. "Morgaine! Stop exercising and unhex this goddamn Rubik's Cube right now!"

"What's that?" Morgaine cups her ears.

"You heard me."

"Just let me finish. I'm in a zone." She backflips again.

Once.

Twice.

Electricity crackles around her and POOF!

Morgaine vanishes in a flash of purple smoke, leaving the rest of us coughing in her wake. Rubbing my eyes, I survey the empty gym and the shocked faces of my companions.

Mordred waves the smoke from his face. "Did my mother just... disappear by backflip?"

"Sorry to tell you this, kid," I say, recalling the time Morgaine backflipped out a tower window. "This isn't the first time."

24

Okay. Don't panic.

Things could be worse. *A lot* worse.

Remember the time Morgaine hacked my Instagram account and uploaded Merlin's amateur photos on my feed? I'd lost 85K subscribers *and* my Ainsley Mills brand deal because of ugly aesthetics. *That* was the *literal* worst thing Morgaine could have done to me.

Morgaine disappearing in a puff of purple smoke like she's freaking Harry Houdini and stranding me with an unsolvable Rubik's Cube containing 1/7th of my soul? Small fries. She's wronged me so much in the past, it's like, how do you choose which offense is worse? Morgaine deserves a top ten Listicle.

After the smoke clears, Vicky stands in the middle of the gym with her hands propped on her hip. Her shrewd eyes scan every inch of gym equipment in case Morgaine is hiding behind the treadmill.

"Where did she disappear to this time?" Vicky asks.

Merlin and I exchange a knowing look.

"If I know le Fey," Merlin says, "she's back in London. That witch has one thing on her mind."

"The throne of England." Vicky shakes her head. "She's a broken record. So we go to London?" A pause. "In 1987?"

"She can be anywhere," Merlin says. "In any time."

Vicky rolls her eyes. "And she never stays in one place."

Mordred snorts. "I'd say..."

"So that's it? She's treating the time-space continuum like her personal amusement park! But won't she need me?" I ask. "I'm the queen in Operation Royal Takeover. I'm *the one*."

"She *has* you," Merlin says, taking the Rubik's Cube from me and holding it up to the fluorescent lights. "1/7th of your soul."

The Cube diffracts rays of neon purple light through the gym and looks like the most evil '80s cursed object ever.

I sit down on a bench. "I'm starting to think sharing my soul is a bad idea."

Vicky and Merlin shoots me a look that says 'you think?'

"Where the fuck did she go?" I ask the empty gym.

My question yields blank expressions.

"She could be in Egypt or France for all we know. She's like Carmen Sandiego," Vicky says.

"Who is Carmen Sandiego?" Merlin whispers.

"Only my favorite video game," Mordred says.

"What's a video game?"

Mordred rakes his hands through his half-mullet. "Come on, man..."

I sigh, gut punched. I don't relish chasing Morgaine through different continents and different times. Chances are she won't make it easy for me. Don't tell me I'll have to wait for Morgaine to contact me via a stupid burner phone like last time. It was highly inefficient and old school. I couldn't even hear her over the static and we had scheduling conflicts that almost screwed up theme park Sunday. What we had was a failure to communicate.

Mordred joins me on the bench and drapes an arm over my shoulder. Gross. I shrug him off and scoot away.

"Mind my personal space, kid."

He shoots me a cocksure grin. "I know where she is."

25

"No way," I say in response to Mordred's guess. "She would *never* return to her time. Why would she trade electricity, plumbing, and aerobics for cold smelly castles and chauvinistic men?"

Merlin, one of the chauvinistic men in question, whirls on Mordred. "Are you sure?"

"Yeah," Mordred rubs his palms together, "Mother's always going on and on about making things right."

"What things?" Merlin asks.

"I don't know," Mordred shrugs. "Things with my father?"

"Arthur. All roads lead back to Arthur." I shake my head and level Merlin with a stern look. "See what happens when you don't provide your baby mama/half-sister with child support?"

Shooting me a glare, Merlin begins to pace. "But why now?"

Vicky joins him in pacing. "She's got something up her sleeve!"

Together they canvas the gym mats, diverging off into their separate corners and converging at a central point before the wall of mirrors.

Vicky checks her hair. "Why trick you into giving her 1/7th of your soul unless she plans to..."

"Lay claim to the throne herself." Merlin strokes his chin.

"Using what?"

"Part of Laurel Kirby."

"To do what?"

Merlin snaps his fingers. "Yank Excalibur from the stone, ensure her claim is uncontested, and kill Arthur!"

I follow their deductions like a volleyball match.

"In order to do that," I say, trying to wrap my mind around this bizarre situation, "Morgaine would have to time travel to *before* Arthur's had a chance to pull the sword from the stone. She'll cut in front of Arthur, take Excalibur using my influencer mojo, and legitimize her claim as Queen of the Britons."

Merlin and Vicky turn to me. *Bingo.*

"That's basically what Merlin just said."

"But it's so fucked up that it's worth repeating!" I pound my palm with my fist. "So you're saying she doesn't need me?"

"She's cut you out," Vicky says, "you're the middleman."

"That's so cold!"

Mordred shrugs. "That's my mother. She does what she wants."

I yank out my phone and pull up MorgVNP. "Not on my watch."

26

THE FOUR OF us huddle on the rooftop of the hotel. Miami shimmers before us in a neon sea. We're dressed in our most neutral outfits so we can blend in with the locals. After I filled Vicky and Mordred in on my clash with the serfs, they were quick to ditch their '80s clothes and accessories.

"I'm keeping my blazer with the shoulder pads," Vicky says. "And if any of those racist villagers try to attack me with their gardening equipment, I'm going to show them what I learned in after school karate."

In demonstration, she jumps into the air and does three roundhouse kicks in quick succession like she's freaking Jean-Claude Van Damme. There's nothing up here for her to kick, so she lands on her feet and slaps her hands together.

"Show off," I say.

Both Merlin and Mordred steps back from my cousin, ghost white with shock.

"Vicky and I took after-school karate for five years. I never got farther than a green belt, but Vicky got her black belt. You do *not* want to mug her in a dark alley."

Mordred looks Vicky up and down, his gaze lingering on her ass. "Damn."

"Not the time to be a pig, kid," I say, swatting him on the back. He's been quiet during the whole ordeal and has dialed back his obnoxious swagger. "How much do you remember of the Dark Ages?"

"Arthurian Ages," Vicky corrects.

"Tomato tom*aaa*to," I say.

"Not much," he says. "I was a baby and then we relocated for my education."

"When did you grow up?"

"In the '70's."

"Then this is new to you too," I say, rolling up my sleeves. "Never fear, I used to be an influencer in King Arthur's court, which makes me the cultural expert here."

Merlin clears his throat.

"Oh right," I say, blushing. "Merlin knows a thing or two about Camelot as well. He's second in command."

I motion for everyone to gather around as I type in the date on my phone.

Merlin takes my phone, dials back to the correct date, and hands the phone back to me.

"Thanks Merlin. *Whew.* Wouldn't want to go *there*!"

See? That's why I need Merlin as my time traveling companion. Without him, I *literally* won't know where I'd be.

I clear my throat and sheepishly glance around. "Everyone ready?"

Three heads nod. Mordred gives me a thumbs up. "Ready, Boss."

Boss? I'm liking the kid more and more.

We join hands. "Hold on to your butts," I say, and press 'Done.'

I WAKE up with my face in the mud.

My ears ring and my head feels like it's been pummeled by not one, but *two* hard sole flip-flops. One on each side of my skull. *Thwack. Thwack.*

Around me, I heard excited voices in rough British accents and jaunty flute music.

Someone steps on me. I jolt awake. It's the flutist, dressed in a green jerkin and red tights, and soft pointy elf shoes with bells on the tips.

"Yo! Watch where you're going!"

The flutist shakes his bell shoes and jig-hops away without apologizing.

"Asshole." Still clutching my aching head, I survey my surroundings. I'm sprawled in a muddy road, right in the middle of foot traffic.

Hundreds of people dressed in reds, blues, and greens stream past me. Men in leather jerkins, fur coats, and silk tights. Women in long velvet dresses and gigantic headpieces of all shapes and sizes. I spot a few ladies going for the Maleficent look with double-coned headpieces. No one in the crowd smells particularly nice, but I caught a strong whiff of clove and cinnamon amongst the body odor.

A woman presses a handkerchief to her nose, muttering about how the constable needs to do something about the drunks and beggars.

I scramble to my feet.

Where the hell am I?

This isn't the Camelot I remember, yet it's not the sad serf village either.

I'm surrounded on both sides by a mismatch of structures crammed together. The facades are patched with mud, clay, horsehair, and straw. A three-story house is the tallest on the block and has an A-frame hay roof.

I assume I've landed in London? Right in the middle of a festival?

I join the surging crowd as they follow the Pied Piper toward a courtyard in front of a grand cathedral.

I check over my shoulder for my time traveling companions. No familiar faces. I've landed in the middle of a busy city street and was trampled by foot traffic. What if my companions fared far worse? Oh dear God... Suppose they've been trampled by horses or were mugged, stabbed, and left dying in the street?

Wooden wheels creak. A cow bell rings close behind me. The crowd parts as an ox cart plows through the middle of the thoroughfare. I'm about to move aside when the cart slams into the back of my legs, toppling me backward onto a funky pile of hay.

Oh hell no! I've been scooped up! Kidnapped in the Medieval equivalent of a white van.

"What do you think you're doing?!" I scramble to my knees and whip my head around. My jaw drops. "Merlin?"

Merlin, dressed in a brown leather jacket with rough stitches and a blue skull cap, is pushing the ox cart. He presses a finger to his lips and winks at me.

"Got it." In a daze, I survey the inside of the cart and spot a pile of bodies. Two conscious, two passed out. "Vicky? Mordred?"

"Help me with this dress," Vicky says, peeling a blue dress away from an unconscious woman.

"Hey Laurel." Mordred yanks on the boots of the unconscious man.

My attention falls on the victims. They appear to have been bopped on the head. I'm only too well acquainted with Merlin's method of acquiring period appropriate clothes, but I expected better of Vicky.

The unconscious man stirs.

"Quiet, you!" Mordred conks him on the head with the hilt of a stolen dagger.

At least Mordred is acting in line with expectation. He tosses me a bundle. "We stole a dress for you."

With a frown, I eye the *two* bodies. I don't see a third. I unfold the dress, bright green and frumpy, non-aesthetic and a little on the smelly side. I wrinkle my nose. "You shouldn't have."

"Don't worry," Mordred says. "I didn't even have to knock this chick out."

I turn to Vicky for explanation. "He bought this woman a drink at the pub and the next thing you know, she's handing over her clothes to him."

"Mordred! What did you say to her?"

He shrugs as if women stripping for him was no big deal.

The people are abuzz in an atmosphere of gaiety and some have already taken to the drink. Slurred greetings and huzzahs ring above the flute music.

As we near the courtyard, we're greeted by the sizzle of roast pork and the clomping of hooves. All around us people swig tankards of mead while girls, adorned in floral headpieces, dance around a maypole.

"What's going on?" I ask. "A holiday? A festival?"

"A joust," Merlin says, motioning us out of the ox cart. He

yanks off his skull cap and nods toward a little hill removed from the merrymaking. Excalibur is stuck in a waist-high piece of black granite. "And a kingmaking."

28

<hr>

WE CANVAS the festival in search of Morgaine. She could be anywhere, riding anything, dressed as anyone. By now, I fully expect her to arrive in purple.

Merlin calls dibs on joust arena surveillance while Mordred and Vicky, both newbs to this time period, are on the buddy system and tasked with scoping out the food stalls. Not that I envy them. The food here turns my stomach (does the head of a peacock sewn onto the rump of a pig sound *appetizing* to you?) and could do with more seasoning.

I'm hiding out in the stables near the famous Excalibur and keeping my eyes peeled for signs of Morgaine.

The stable is dark and cool, all the best stallions have been moved to the jousting arena, with the exception of one gentle mare that neighs and nickers as if to say 'boys are dumb.'

"Yeah, they are," I answer back and try, for the thousandth time, to solve the hexed Rubik's Cube.

Did you know that solving a Rubik's Cube involves a series of algorithms? That's my secret to solving it so fast the first time. As an influencer, I live and die by algorithms and sometimes (okay, *most* of the time), it's all I can think of.

I'm not a genius, but one of the perks of being algorithm obsessed is solving a Rubik's Cube in record time. But this is what I can't figure out:

I'm twisting and turning the damn thing, and the same algorithm no longer applies. It's really and truly hexed.

What if I can't unhex it?

Morgaine may have 1/7th of my soul, but I have 1/7th of her powers.

Yes. That's it. I'm totally going to unhex the shit out of this Rubik's Cube.

"Maybe I *am* a genius?" I say to the empty stables.

"Neigh," the mares says, sounding disagreeable.

"Who asked you?"

Setting the Rubik's Cube on a bale of hay, I charge up my hands (sorceress hands are like iPhones. They run out of power so fast after a while) and prepare to unhex this '80s Horcrux when someone dashes through the stables and ruins my concentration.

Cursing under my breath, I pocket the Cube and poke my head out to investigate.

Up on the hill, a boy with golden hair is sneaking toward Excalibur.

My heart skips a beat. It's Arthur. A few years younger, but King Arthur of freaking Camelot and my future boss. We were close. I painted his portrait and gave him the best goddamn haircut of his life.

His ugly bowl cut is back (because he hasn't met me yet) and his tunic is shabby and more patched up than Ainsley Mill's Winter line of distressed denim. He's scrawny and scared, a shadow of the athletic king I knew... will meet. Actually, he can't be a shadow of a king until he's become king and then aged out, grown a beer gut, and talks about his glory days. So what does that make him now? A sapling? Time traveling is confusing, but I digress.

Young sapling Arthur is as jumpy as a squirrel as he creeps toward the sword in the stone.

I silently cheer Arthur on like a proud mom as he gazes upon Excalibur with awe. The clouds part and a ray of light beams down from the heavens, bathing both boy and sword in a golden glow. It's a great photo op. You can't buy filters like that. In fact, someone should replicate this moment as a Lightroom preset and sell them as "God filters." Maybe that someone should be me...

I raise my phone and snap a few photos. Arthur has a derpy look on his face and his big blue eyes shine with wonder. It's Hallmark movie poster face if I ever saw one (not my aesthetic. I'm more into Merlin's smoldering serial killer stare) but I can work with it.

As I'm framing my composition, a purple shadow steals across the hill, blocking out the sun.

The clouds open up and the heavens rumble. A dark bundle drops from the sky and lands next to Arthur.

The boy stumbles away from Excalibur. Arthur is shook.

*I* am shook.

The mysterious visitor unfurls herself like a vampire bat, her purple velvet cloak swishing around her like a swirl of smoke. Her raven mane is no longer teased like she's the hot teacher in an '80s hair band music video, but straight and sleek. When she lifts her head, I notice she's eased up on the smoky eye and purple highlighter, but her cheekbones are still on point and I'd recognize that smug smirk anywhere. I want to slap her face.

"Morgaine," I mutter under my breath. "Don't you dare!"

## 29

ARTHUR SHIELDS his eyes and takes a tentative step forward. "Morgaine?"

She tips her head to the side. "My little brother," she says in a tone that sends the hackles rising on the back of my neck. Morgaine unfolds her cloak some more, revealing a vampy blood-red corset with purple laces.

I wrinkle my nose. She's done it this time. She's gone full goth.

"How did you fall from the sky?" Arthur asks.

"Did you notice that too?" Morgaine says, swishing around her cloak.

"There's something different about you," Arthur narrows his eyes. "You look... old."

His comment wipes the smirk from her face. Ha!

Losing patience, Morgaine steps forward, sorceress hands at the ready.

Uh-oh. I've seen that claw formation before. I know what it's capable of: lightning blasts, tentacle-conjuring, shrinkage... Morgaine's powers are a mystery bag of horrors. Shit's about to get real.

I break cover and charge forward, ready to cast a neon pink net over Morgaine. Or maybe I'll shrink her too. I haven't decided yet. Actually, I can never predict what comes out of my fingers just like I can never plan what I want for breakfast. That's why it baffles me when Merlin claims he lived in a cave during his formative years, just so he could learn how to move a broom with his mind. I've been a sorceress for all of three days, and I can *totally* move a broom or reach out and grab my phone from a nightstand. I'm not saying I'm a better sorceress... Come to think of it, moving things around is a great idea!

I wax circles in the air. I'm going to move the shit out of Morgaine, but she's too fast for me.

Without warning, Morgaine body slams Arthur and pushes him to the ground like a playground bully.

"You bloody hag!" Arthur says, nursing his sore shoulder.

"Shut it." Morgaine kicks him in the nuts, smiling as he writhes on the ground.

Shrugging off her cloak, Morgaines turns her attention to Excalibur and cracks her knuckles. She straightens her shoulders and *looks straight* at me.

I halt in my tracks. A tingle worms its way through me. Gross. I can *feel* Morgaine peeping inside me and tapping into my soul powers. It's super invasive and violating. My flesh breaks out into goosebumps.

With a smug tilt of her head, Morgaine grasps the sword hilt.

"Gah!" I glance down and flex my palms.

I *feel* the sword. She's using me to yank Excalibur out of the stone! Our powers are... *combining.* Stop it! Stop! Our powers should never mix.

"Oi!" a man cries. "That woman has Excalibur! She's going to claim the sword! Let's watch!"

The festival goers race en mass to watch the spectacle. I run ahead of them and beat them to the hill. Soon the eyewitnesses will see Morgaine take the sword and crown her queen. No way is she going to use my special powers and claim all the credit. Not on my watch!

Summoning up all my willpower, I shut every door and window inside of myself and lock Morgaine out. I can't keep her out for long, just long enough to stop her and carry out my plan.

Morgaine tugs on Excalibur and when the sword doesn't budge, she glares at me. Her expression promises murder.

I know I don't have long. With a raging war cry, I charge her and knock her to the ground. She lands beside Arthur.

I have a slim window before Morgaine recovers and sinks her vengeful claws into my back. Time to hustle.

"Here goes nothing..." I grasp Excalibur and yank with all my might.

And really... All the fuss about Excalibur being impossible to remove? Exaggeration! I didn't need to try that hard because Excalibur comes out as easily as if someone had lubed up the blade with WD-40.

A cheer ripples through the crowd.

Everyone claps. Men in tights. Women in horn hats. Even the flutist who stepped on me. They're all mad for me. It's like my pulling the sword out of the stone earned me ten thousand Likes. My heart swells with pride and good will toward my fellow man, woman, or gender neutral friends. I can't wait to wave and strut Excalibur around for the sheer theater of it all.

But first...

I reach into my pocket and plop the Rubik's Cube on the stone.

"Laurel!" Morgaine's eyes widen in horror. She reaches for me. "Don't you dare!"

"I do what I want!" With another Amazonian cry (I'm quite good at these), I raise Excalibur and slam it down on the Rubik's Cube.

What happens next is pure chaos:

Colored squares sailing everywhere, 1/7th of my soul docking with the mothership, 1/7th of my sorceress powers slowly slipping from my body and docking with Morgaine's mothership... And Morgaine, now furious as fuck, shocking me with lightning and the crowd, my people, booing her while cheering me on.

I'm suspend in mid-air, my legs planted apart, Excalibur raised above my head *'Masters of the Universe'* style. My body is outlined in neon purple light as I spasm out. I don't know how many purple lightning strikes I can stand before I die.

"Somebody stop her!" I grit my teeth. "She's totally going to kill me!"

Suddenly Morgaine relinquishes me from her grasp. I collapse onto the stone, Excalibur still clutched in my hands. It takes me a while to recover, but when I finally come to, I turn to see that Arthur has tackled Morgaine to the ground.

"I've got her!" he yells, then yelps as she head butts him and scrambles out of his grasp.

"The witch!" The spectators yell. "She's free!"

"Get the constable!"

"No! A constable can't detain her."

There's a scramble. Then a chase. "She's fast!"

"She's headed toward the woods!"

I poke my head up in time to see Morgaine elude her captors. She's fleet of foot and fast as a hare, mad-dashing toward the forest where she'll disappear for good. Just as she's about to break through the dark fringe of elms, she freezes. Her body arches backward and she spasms as if she's being electrocuted. She's wrapped from head to toe in a neon blue lasso, which happens to be zapping the living hell out of her.

Morgaine le Fey falls to her knees, her arms reaching for the sky, her mouth spewing all manners of foul words.

Raising myself to my feet, I turn to Morgaine's captor or shall I say... *captors.*

Hot Merlin is holding one end of the magic lasso, but someone equally delicious holds onto the other end: Hot Merlin.
    "Holy shit! Two Merlins!"

## 30

Hot Merlin, that is, *my* Merlin, is conversing with his younger and equally hot self. I'd like to note that it doesn't take much effort for Merlin to convince himself that time traveling is a thing and go over the whole spiel of why we're here, introductions, handshakes, sexy side eyes to me (more on this later).

I'm impressed by how Young Merlin is so accepting of this whole thing, and I wonder if this isn't the craziest thing the Merlins have seen. Maybe the Merlins have a safe word. Okay. I'm totally going to have a safe word with myself if I ever time travel back two years ago. My word with be super legit and uncrackable. Or who says it should even be a word? How about a number? 125K. The number of Instagram followers I had before Morgaine hacked my account and ruined my life. But Laurel of two years ago didn't have 125K followers, so if I ever meet myself, I'll blow my own mind.

But I digress.

*Holy shit.* The Merlins have taken down Morgaine! This just goes to show that *two* wizards are better than one.

"Get your hands off of me!" Morgaine squirms in her magic bindings, her words muffled by the neon blue muzzle both

Merlins strapped over her mouth. Guess she called them 'cock-suckers' one too many times.

Together, the Merlins haul their struggling package through the jeering crowd and toss her in the back of an ox-cart.

"Where are they taking her?" Vicky asks.

"To the dungeons," Mordred says and spits on the ground.

Whoa! Vick and I jump back. Gross.

"Good riddance." Mordred mutters something about wishing to be involved in Morgaine's torture when Young Arthur, nuts recovered, joins our group.

"I suspect they'll just lock her up with a crust of bread and water," Arthur says. "We don't hold much with torture here. I can show you where the dungeon is if visiting is what you want."

Mordred steps back, his complexion pale, his mouth slack. He grasps for speech. It isn't every day you meet your future dead beat father/uncle.

I poke Vicky in the ribs. "I suspect Mordred is having a moment." I clear my throat. "Mordred, would you like to visit the dungeons with Arthur? You can taunt Morgaine together."

Vicky hides a smile. "And play catch afterward?"

"Catch what?" Arthur asks.

"A baseball," I say. "Oh right, you don't have baseballs. What kind of balls do you have? Wait... don't answer that."

Arthur reddens. "We toss hammers."

That's weird. Of all the silly things to toss... No, Laurel. No judgement. "There you go! Mordred... hammers?"

The kid swallows. "I'd like that."

My heart melts as I watch father and son follow the ox-cart to the dungeon.

I let out a huge sigh. "Medieval people can be so sweet."

"Technically, we're not in the Medieval Ages," Vicky points out.

"Tomato *Tomaaaato.*"

"That being said," she adds with a humble tilt of her head,

"before this I didn't even know there was an Arthurian Age. Didn't even know the dude existed, so that goes to show what I know."

"Do you realize, Vic," I say, patting her on the back, "that this is the first time you've ever made sense?"

Vicky rolls her eyes. "Whatever, Laurel."

I breathe a sigh of relief. "It's over."

I have my soul back. Morgaine is in jail. Merlin has returned to his own time, which sucks on many levels, but I'm still confident that I can convince him to time travel with me. I hoist Excalibur over my shoulder, intent on returning it back to the stone for Arthur to grab.

"You!" A man calls from the crowd.

I halt with sword mid-raised. "Me?"

"Yes, you!" he points at me. "What is your name?"

All heads turn to me. I swallow. "Um... Laurel Kirby?"

A thousand voices murmur my name.

*'Tis a strange name.*

*Mayhaps because it's a special name.*

"You're the one!" a woman cries. "You freed the sword from the stone! I saw it with me own eyes!"

"Aye," an old man seconds. "She plucked the sword from the stone like a needle."

"I was just... It's Arthur you want. He loosened it for me."

"Who's Arthur?" the crowd asks.

"He's..." *Damn it.* I shouldn't have sent him off with Mordred.

"The sword has spoken! We have a new queen!"

I turn to my wide-eyed cousin. "No, no! There's a misunderstanding!"

"There's no misunderstanding about it!" another fellow yells. "You are the Once and Future Queen." He raises a fist in the air. "Long live Queen Laurel!"

"Long live Queen Laurel!"

"Vicky!" I lower my voice. "What do I do?"

"Who are you?" someone asks Vicky.

Vicky steps forward, head held at a haughty angle. "I'm her cousin and her lawyer."

A murmur of confusion and then someone yells, "The queen's counsel!"

The crowd swells around me. Trumpeters herald the new proclamation and the people start to dance. The flutist strikes up a merry tune and skips along, leading the crowd back to the castle.

Hands grab me and hoist me in the air. I'm passed amongst my subjects. People stop by and kiss my Ainsley Mills rose gold signet ring. Women hold up their babies for blessings.

"Hip Hip Huzzah!"

"Hip Hip Huzzah!"

"No!" I bounce across the sea of hands, searching for Vicky. She's crowd surfing behind me and enjoying it more than I am. "I'm not a queen. I'm just an influencer!" My protests are drowned out by exuberant chanting.

*"Her Majesty is humble!"*

*"We are truly blessed."*

*"It is the beginning of a new age!"*

*"The Age of Laurel!"*

*"Hip Hip Huzzah!"*

*"Hip Hip Huzzah!"*

*"Long live the queen!"*

*"Long live the queen!"*

## 31

I DOWN MY seventh goblet of mead. My banquet seat is cushioned (Thank God) by a velvet butt pillow, but not much else.

Page boys set silver platter after silver platter of meat before me. Roast squab and stuffed geese. Wild boar and mountain goat. I take a bite of everything so as not to offend the chef, but after my twelfth plate of meats, I'm thinking about becoming a vegetarian.

"Where's the vegetable dish?" I ask one of page boys.

His brows furrow in confusion. "Vegetables, Your Majesty?"

"You know, greens? Salad? Green beans? Carrots? Broccoli? Kale?"

The page gulps and points to a small plate of gooey gray mush that no one has touched. "Turnips, ma'am."

My stomach turns. I regret not packing a blender in my trusty time-traveling tote bag. My kingdom for a green smoothie! If I want a balanced diet, seems like I'll have to venture into the forest and forage for my own vegetables.

The entertainment line up involves jugglers during the fish course. The juggler isn't very good. He can only handle three balls at once. A fourth is overkill. The juggler is the opening act to the main event: a jester who specializes in culturally insensitive jokes and farts on command.

Afterward, I open gifts from all the rulers of Europe to celebrate my reign as queen.

"This one's cute," I say, nodding at a gold birdcage, "but I don't have a bird."

I spoke too soon. A man enters the Great Hall with a cage packed to the brim with exotic birds. It sounds like the opening line of a bad joke and looks like a scene from *Aladdin*. Personally, I don't think it's sanitary to bring twenty birds to a banquet hall.

I shift in my seat. Please don't tell me this dude is planning to release them for spectacle. What if they shit on our heads?

"...Surely these do not all belong to me."

"Every beak and feather belongs to you, Your Majesty."

"Great," I murmur to Vicky. As royal advisor, she sits at my right hand. "What do I do with all these birds?"

"You select a few as pets," she says.

"But they do not all fit in the cage. What happens to the rest?"

Merlin whispers in my left ear. "We eat them."

I whirl on him in horror. "Oh, hell no!" I eye the chirping birds. "They are too colorful to eat."

"The more colorful, the better. The cook will bake them in a pie for you."

"Gross," Vicky and I say in unison.

Merlin leans back. His profile is immediately replaced by Young Merlin, who salutes me with a goblet of mead.

Ever since Merlin met himself, the two have become inseparable BFFs. And if the kingdom thinks it's strange that there's now *two* Merlins, no one has mentioned anything. Everyone probably thinks Merlin has found his long-lost twin, and it's so adorable how they coordinate their robes and finish each other's sentences. Two hot wizards, one mind.

"It's a popular coronation dish," Young Merlin says.

"Arthur used to love birds in a pie," OG Merlin adds.

Young Merlin does a double take. "The skinny squire?"

"Aye," Merlin tells himself. "He is the boy who *would* have been king had Laurel Kirby...er, Her Majesty, not intervened."

"I cannot imagine it." Young Merlin strokes his chiseled chin. "I cannot fathom anyone who is more fit for the crown."

I blush. "Thanks, Young Hot Merlin."

"I can," OG Merlin mutters.

I shoot him a dirty look and he quickly glances away.

Okay.

OG Merlin has been throwing shade at me all evening. He's still bitter about yesterday's outcome and firmly in Arthur's corner. It's not like I planned to take the throne away from the kid! I was trying to defeat Morgaine, and I ended up queen as an accident.

Seriously. OG Merlin's anger at me is unfounded.

I would totally give up the throne, but the good people of Briton won't hear of it. They love their queen. Now that I'm on the throne, it's hard to give it up. I can see what Morgaine is talking about. Absolute power is awesome. I like being liked. Everyone loves me. Everyone except the one person who's supposed to be my most loyal supporter.

I don't like Merlin's attitude.

Ever since my coronation, he's been doubting my choices left and right.

Do I *really* want mink on my robe? Wouldn't I rather have white fox fur?

Am I sure I don't want Morgaine tortured with hot oil?

Am I sure I want to change the tapestries in the round table room?

Is Vicky *really* qualified to be my royal advisor? What are her references? Dude! He knows Vicky. She didn't get into Harvard, but she took a summer class there in the summer of 'II. That's good enough for me.

Now I know why Henry VIII was so ax happy. When your advisors doubt every decision you make, you're bound to snap.

And don't let me get started about how he mansplained the workings of the twelve knight fellowship. Just wait until I tell him I plan to get rid of the round table (big ugly Medieval furniture isn't my thing) in favor of an open planned office with standing desks. He'll bust a vein.

OG Merlin notices me tapping my fingers on my arm rest. "There's still time to resign," he whispers in my ear. "And let the rightful king take his place."

My blood boils. "What makes you think I want to resign?"

"Laurel Kirby—"

"It's *Your Majesty* to you."

"Apologies. *Your Majesty*... Ruling England is a trying job, filled with responsibilities and decisions that are beyond your scope of comprehension."

"Are you saying I'm too stupid to rule England?"

"The words never left my mouth."

"But you don't think I'm 'responsible' enough for the job?"

Merlin shrugs. "I question your judgement."

"I can have your head for this!"

He arches an eyebrow, calling my bluff. "Will you?"

I slump on my royal cushion as page boys bring me a platter of lavender and rosewater marzipan. "I don't believe in the death penalty," I say, digging into the sweets. "Mark my words, I can totally rock this monarch thing. Unlike other rulers, I plan to change things up and get shit done."

Merlin shakes his head. "Being Queen of England is not a thing to be taken lightly."

I take a swig from my bejeweled goblet and shrug my shoulders. "Like it's hard."

## 32

OKAY. Confession: I don't know shit about being Queen of England. But I'm not going to let that problem stop me from trying.

To tell the truth, during the first week of my reign, I was having *major* imposter syndrome. Like who am I to think I can rule a kingdom and bring peace amongst warring factions and lead my people in a Holy Crusade? That's pretty big shoes to fill.

I tossed and turned for seven straight nights, my bear fur comforter tangled around my ankles as I stared up at my royal canopy. How did Arthur do it? When I became his court influencer, he was *literally* a kid and yet so much responsibility fell upon his shoulder.

For days, I was super stressed and filled with self-doubt. I think I might have developed not one, but *three* wrinkles on my forehead. Plagued by anxiety-induced insomnia, I pulled up my phone and browsed my Instagram for strength.

What does it mean to be a leader? So many people look to me for fashion and lifestyle advice... how do I translate my voice into fair and just rule?

Suppose I fail and the *huzzahs* stop... leading to an insurrection? A revolution? Suppose I end up with my head in a basket like Marie Antoinette? In my defense, I would never tell my people to eat cake. The last thing this kingdom needs is more carbs. The serfs have a protein deficiency, and if it were up to me, everyone could do with more meat. And vegetables. Let them drink kale protein smoothies.

Wait.

It *is* up to me!

That was the *exact* moment my imposter syndrome disappeared. And seriously, it didn't take that long. See what you can accomplish by scrolling your phone in the middle of the night?

Energized and inspired, I summoned a servant for a quill, ink, and parchment. I tipped the page boy a gold coin (it's important to tip your child servants), flexed my fingers, and got to work.

I'm prepared to work all night. It only takes half an hour. Outlining the doctrines of fair and just rule doesn't really take that long. Wikipedia tells me it took ten grueling months for the founding fathers to write the U.S. Constitution. What the heck were they doing? Knitting afghans?

Plopping my quill in its ink pot, I summon Vicky to my royal chambers.

She arrives grouchy, scratching her rump. She's dressed in a velvet robe, her hair wrapped in curling ribbons. "It's the middle of the freaking night."

You would think she would speak to me with a little more respect now that I'm queen, but that's Vicky for you.

"Look, Vicky! I've outlined some improvements for Camelot." I hand her my masterpiece.

She reads the title: "Queen Laurel's Totally Awesome Magna Carta?"

I nod, beaming. "It's totally awesome, right?"

Vicky frowns at the parchment, then pulls up a chair. "I think I need to sit down for this."

## 33

**QUEEN LAUREL's Totally Awesome Magna Carta**

1. We hold these truths to be self evident that all men and women, men who identify as women and vice versa (see amendments for the all-inclusive umbrella) of any color and creed are created equal.

2. Land and inheritance is passed down to whoever you think worthy. Example: if your worthless first-born son can't work a plow or balance the books, leave the farm/castle to your smarter daughter/son/cousin/neighbor, etc...

3. Be excellent to each other. (Queen Laurel came up with this herself and was in no way influenced by Bill and Ted).

4. Don't be an asshole. Examples of assholes: Morgaine le Fey.

Amendment: all persons found guilty of being an asshole will be jailed in the castle dungeons, given a ration of bread and water, and subject to a public shaming.

5. War? What is it good for? Absolutely nothing. Make love not war... but *don't* make love to your close relations if you can help it, unless it makes you happy, in which case, wake up to birth control because ain't nobody got time to deal with your incest baby.

Amendment to Law #5: all subjects of Camelot must attend Sunday classes on birth control methods after church services. Sheep gut condoms and sundry will be provided by your friar/vicar/priest. Refreshments also included!

6. That old rule about women and dowries? Fuck that. From this day forward, no woman shall be required to pay lazy, broke-ass men for the privilege of marrying them.

7. Serf villages and dwellings will be subject to a deep clean on the 3rd Tuesday of every month. All ox carts and horses parked on the street between the hours of 8 am -12 pm will be subject to tow.

8. Seven laws are plenty. Ain't nobody got time to write eight.
   *Note to town crier: don't read this aloud.*

"... ain't nobody got time to write eight rules," Vicky reads to the masses and then stops dead as she realizes her error. She peers over the scroll at my red face. "Oops. Sorry."

We turn to my subjects, waiting for their reaction. Silence falls on the kingdom, followed by murmuring voices.

I adjust the golden clasp on my snow fox fur cloak and shift in my soft royal slippers.

"Oh shit," I whisper to Vicky. "Do you think my Magna Carta was too shocking? Is the street sweeping bit too much?"

"It's not how I would have worded it," Vicky says, staring down at my seven laws. "Maybe I've been hit too many times on the head, but your Magna Carta actually makes sense. It's just... here it is. Very direct. No bullshit."

"Yes, but does it make sense to the people?" I gasp as a horrible thought pops into my mind. "Is my re-election in danger?"

"Your seat on the throne is secure," Young Merlin says over my left shoulder. "You are queen until you die."

"Or until another monarch kills you and takes your throne,"

OG Merlin says with that familiar skeptical notch between his brows. "What's this about 'make love not war?'"

"I don't think it needs an explanation," I say. "It means what it means. It's not that deep."

"In her simplicity," Young Merlin winks at me, "Her Majesty is the most deep."

OG Merlin scowls at Young Merlin. Can you be at odds with yourself? Apparently Merlin can.

Young Merlin is much more impressed by my ideas than OG Merlin, who seems to be a secret war hawk. He's always on me about defending Britain's borders against the Saxons and Vikings and trying to get me to beef up our armies for the Crusades.

No!

No Crusades! Camelot doesn't have time to divert precious resources and man power to fight a war. We've got plenty of trouble here at home...

Like that leper colony by the mountain side. Holy shit! Have you seen these people? They have no *noses* and are living in hovels with no plumbing or aesthetic decor. We need to get a medic over there ASAP and treat these poor folks before another piece of their face falls off.

I'm up to my elbows in famine, poverty, and Medieval plumbing issues and Merlin wants to ship able-bodied men over to the East and start a fight. Talk about needing to get his priorities in order.

What part of 'make love not war' does he not understand? That being said, he's going to throw a shit fit once he finds out my stance of 'No Crusades.' If he challenges me, I might have to throw him in the dungeons with Morgaine.

Meanwhile, Young Merlin is much easier to work with, probably because he's living in a whole new timeline where I'm queen and the world isn't ravaged by plagues (see Law #7 in Public Sanitation of the serf villages), women aren't oppressed (Law #1 and

#6), and Europe isn't ravaged by wars (Law #5). See what I mean about getting shit done? It's like I know what I'm doing...

After a long bout of silence, one man in the crowd claps. His clap is joined by another and another until all of Camelot is clapping.

"I like it!" someone says.

"It's easy to understand!"

"I like things you don't have to think too much about!"

"Our Queen is fair and learned!"

"Hers is the voice of the people!"

"The People's Queen!"

"Her Majesty is a genius!"

"Is there nothing Her Majesty can't do?"

"Huzzah! Huzzah! Huzzah!"

My eyes mist with tears. I just love it when I get a gold star on my homework.

Basking in the Likes of *my* people, I turn to OG Merlin and fold my arms across my chest. "The People's Queen they call me."

Merlin grimaces. "I heard."

"Do you doubt me now?"

"We shall see how well your Magna Carta fares in practice..."

## 35

VICKY and I were balancing the kingdom's books when two runners burst into the former Round Table room now open plan office.

The runners buckle over, panting and terrified. The more exhausted of the two crashes into a potted ficus (plants are a much better decoration choice than a smelly old tapestry, am I right?).

"Your Majesty!"

"Yes?"

"Invaders to the east," Runner 1 says.

"South East," corrects Runner 2. "The most horrible thing that can happen has happened..."

"A plague the likes of which this kingdom has never seen!"

"The foulest enemy to have reached Briton's shores."

I rap my fingers impatiently on my desk. "Well, spit it out. Who is it?"

"The Saxons, Your Majesty."

An uproar erupts amongst my makeshift parliament.

The two Merlins stand up simultaneously, scraping their chair legs on the stone floor.

Arthur, also a member of my council, pales and reaches for his sword.

Mordred, whom I'd appointed royal apothecary due to his knowledge of certain... *substances*, pumps his fists in the air and mouths "Yes!"

The runners reveal that a small fleet of five ships have landed on the coast and a band of Saxon raiders deployed in-land, razing the land, stealing sheep, and being general assholes.

"Who are the Saxons?" I ask Vicky. "I feel like I should know."

"One minute." Vicky yanks her phone from her portable charger. She scrolls and reads, "The Germans."

"Ah." My shoulder slumps in relief. "I know a little German."

"As do I," Vicky says.

"Think we can brush up in time to welcome them to court?"

"Welcome them to court?!" OG Merlin's eyes bug out of his head.

I frown at Merlin, then drink in the stunned faces all around me. All right. I know what's up. Everyone's expecting me to don my armor, march off to war, and kick Saxon ass.

Tempting as that may be, I've had enough violence to last me a lifetime. Little did they know, I have a better solution up my sleeves.

"Ready the army. Make sure my horse is saddled and cush-ioned," I say. "We march!"

The Merlins nod, satisfied by my command.

"What happened to 'make love not war'?" Vicky asks me as the castle scrambles for a trip to the coast.

I wink. "That's precisely what I plan to do."

It takes three days of grueling travel before we reach the Dover coast.

My entourage is impressive. A thousand men in chain mail and armor bearing my coat of arms. My family doesn't have a coat of arms at the ready, so I designed my own. I went for a woodsy cottage vibe with hanging ivy, a cluster of succulents, and a California mountain lion who is more cute and cuddly than fierce. It's like the perfect Girl Scout badge, though I wouldn't say it strikes fear in the hearts of my enemies. Fear is not what we're after. We want hugs.

I'm sitting astride my horse and decked out in a steal breast plate, chain mail, and knee-high leather boots. My hair whips wildly behind me and I'm pretty sure I look like a warrior princess. I have never felt so empowered in my life. I pity the Saxon who dares to cross me.

From my vantage point atop the limestone cliffs, I peer into a spyglass. Tiny huts dot the pebbled beach. A grey sea mist enshrouds the camp, rendering the invaders hard to see if not for their mighty bulk. A horde of hulking dudes in leather and furs mingle about the beach. They look none too clean or nice. I spot a group attempting to cook fish by a scant fire. A howling sea wind blows out the fire and, hungry and cold, the men gnaw on their catches like grizzly bears.

I hand my spyglass to Arthur, head of my military.

"What shall we do, Your Majesty?" Arthur asks. "Attack from the right? Drive them back to their boats?"

"We take them by surprise," Merlin says, and motions for the army to haul over the catapult he insisted on bringing with us (if it weren't for this blasted catapult, we could have made the journey in two days instead of three. Just sayin').

"We'll douse a boulder with pitch," Merlin's eyes light up with excitement, "light it on fire... they'll never know what hit them."

I stare at Merlin, horrified. "Um... why don't you let me and Vicky handle this?"

The entire army is shook. OG Merlin is about to bust a vein while Arthur stumbles back a step.

"Surely you don't mean to greet the Saxons on your own?!" Arthur says.

"That's exactly what I mean," I say, casting a flinty eye to anyone who dares challenge the wishes of their queen.

OG Merlin clears his throat. "What if you're abducted or worse, killed..."

"I have a hundred archers and two wizards at my back."

"Hmmm."

"We shall be perfectly safe," I swat him on the back, "you underestimate the power of my influence." I nod at Vicky and she gestures to our handlers. "Bring the basket."

In minutes, it's just the two of us riding down to the beach to greet the raiders.

Vicky casts a doubtful glance over her shoulders. "I hope you know what you're doing."

*Me too.* "Have faith in my powers of persuasion."

"That's what I'm afraid of."

A light rain curtains our arrival on the beach. Waves crash against the limestone rock face. We dismount and nearly slip on the slick pebbles underfoot.

"I like Malibu better," Vicky whispers.

"I doubt anyone can get a tan here."

"Anyone who camps out in this frigid wasteland must be into extreme wilderness adventures."

"Total *Patagonia* crowd if they were in our time," I say.

"They strike me more as *North Face* guys," Vicky says.

Our presence stirs the Saxon camp. Soon we're facing a wall of hulking, hostile muscle.

The man to the farthest left heaves an executioner's ax over his shoulder and glares at us beneath heavy brows. His neighbor has a giant caveman club. They both resemble Brick Shithouse (may he rest in peace). In fact, they *all* resemble Brick Shithouse.

Their leader steps forward. He is slighter than his Brick Shithouse army, but only by an inch. A jagged scar slashed across his face. He greets us with a growl.

"Remember our lessons," I whisper to Vicky. "Go for it. Say something."

"Me?" Her eyes widen. "You're the queen. You go first."

With a sigh, I step forward. The leader leaves his men to meet me. I gulp and try to recall my German flashcards. "Guten Morgen!"

The Saxons gawk at me in surprise. A few raise awkward hands and mutter, "Guten Morgen...?"

I raise my hands in welcome and say what I hope is 'Greetings! I am Laurel, Queen of the Briton, and I welcome you with warm hugs and an invitation to a feast at the castle. In honor of your arrival, our cook has roasted bratwurst."

The mention of bratwurst get their attention. I nudge Vicky. "Show them the bratwurst."

She flips open the basket to a collective grunt of approval.

"And look, what's this?" Still working my German, I pick up a stone jar. "How can you eat bratwurst without... coarse ground mustard?"

The Saxons nod to each other. Stomachs growl. A few of the huskier fellows lick their lips.

Sensing the mood shift in his men, the leader asks, "What do you have to drink?"

"Tell them about our beer garden, Vicky."

Vicky clears her throat. In perfect German, she says, "We've commissioned a beer garden in your honor along with all the sausages and potatoes you can eat during your stay. We have a selection of artisan stout and IPA."

"Will the food be spicy?" one of the Saxons asks. "I cannot handle spice."

"The food will be lightly seasoned with salt and pepper," Vicky says, "and the spiciest condiment is the mustard."

The army considers and nods.

"What of the entertainment?" asks a smaller man in the back.

"We have drums and trumpeters, dancing and wenches. Our wenches *choose* to be sex worker as a career and they take great pride in what they do. They are the best wenches — and I totally plan to provide them with health insurance." I clear my throat.

"We also have a flutist who does a solo performance three times a night like clockwork."

"Is he good?" one of the Saxons asks.

Vicky and I share a knowing look. "He's okay," I say, "but he is merry and *very efficient*."

Grunts of approval all around.

"What do you say we ditch this frigid beach and feast as friends?" I hold out my hand to their leader. *"Ja?"*

*"Ja!"* He shakes my hand to the cheering of his men. I look up the cliff and wink at Merlin. See what happens when you make a little effort to be excellent to each other?

Merlin turns away, grumbling.

Laurel: 1

Merlin: 0

## 36

Saxon invaders? Charmed.

Pointless bloody war? Avoided.

Time to clean up this filthy kingdom!

"Really get in there," I say, supervising my newly assembled sanitation crew as they power wash the serf village. "Keep pressure right there. I want to see *white* walls. You've gotta get into the cracks. Really scrape the gunk and grime out of there. Get into the pores."

"Like this, Your Majesty?"

"Yeah, you've got it." I swat the guy on the back.

I trudge along and give shit shoveling tips to the unfortunate soul manning the street sweep. "Put your back into it. Don't be afraid of the poop. *Be* the poop..."

With Merlin's help, we developed a make-shift hose-trolley-donkey system to help cleanse the caked on mud and (literal crap) from the lean-to buildings. It's probably easier to tear down the sad little sheds and rebuild. Unfortunately, our public works budget is stretched thin thanks to the sewage system... and the public bathrooms.

Taking a page from Roman sanitation, we're building a

communal bathroom on a hill for Serf Village A and B consisting of twenty stone holes where you can do your business. The poop is led *away* from the village by way of gravity (shit floats... but not in my kingdom) and BAM! No more offensive smells. No more cholera!

Okay. You may think 'communal bathrooms?' Gross, right? Before I became queen, the serfs were literally squatting and shitting in the streets. We're taking baby steps here.

After a long day of overseeing my public works commission, I stand back to view the fruits of my labor.

The shanty houses are still sad, but now they are shiner. The streets are so clean that people and horses can travel freely without trudging through sludge. Children play in a designated playground area, which consists of a patch of grass... kind of like a dog park. Serfs are lining up to use the communal toilets and I have some guys handing them government issued tree bark. The mood is merry, and I am satisfied by my royal accomplishments. Not since Franklin D. Roosevelt has a ruler done more for public works and a depressed economy.

OG Merlin appears by my side. "It appears your public works commission is a success," he mumbles. "I suppose there's some merit to your Magna Carta."

"What did you say?"

He hangs his head. "You may be right."

I can't help gloating. "You lost a little face, didn't you?"

"I have lost face."

"The serfs are enjoying the toilets." I give them a thumbs up. The serfs in line for the crapper wave their tree barks.

*"Huzzah!"*

*"Huzzah!"*

*"Huzzah!"*

Merlin folds his arms across his chest. "I've never known the peasants to be so happy."

I swat him on the back. "Because you've never provided them with a pleasant way to shit."

"It's uncommon for a queen to visit a leper colony," Guinevere says as she guides me through the mountain pass to see the unfortunates of my kingdom. "Then again," she looks me over with a glint of appreciation, "you are no ordinary queen."

Guinevere, unmarried, is the head of my 'Fight Leprosy' task force. If you remember her from my first trip to Camelot, she was a whiny young queen stuck in an unhappy marriage to a husband who would rather bone his half sister than his wife. She was always on edge, probably because of all the pressure to produce an heir.

"Some babies are beyond saving, poor souls," she tells me, "but we're able to treat eighty percent of the children and their parents."

"Very good," I nod along, as impressed by the task force's progress as I am by the change in Guinevere. She's much more likable now that she has a high-powered job and people to command. I'd even venture to say she's much happier as a single woman than a queen living in Arthur's shadow.

"Here are the caverns," Guinevere says. "As you can see, much improved from last time."

"Much." I shudder at the memory of the first time I toured the leper colony. If I thought the serf village was awful, the leper colony was a sanitation nightmare. Not to mention a moral humiliation for Camelot. Sick, bedraggled people living in dank caves carved in the mountainside. No one, not even the serfs, would have anything to do with them. At first, I was terrified I may catch leprosy, especially when the colony started crawling and limping toward me like a horde of zombies. I began inching away from the moaning crowd, but then it occurred to me that they just wanted my help and it's not their fault that they have creepy zombie vibes. They would walk if they could, but some of them don't have legs. And really, they can't hurt me. I've had my shots and I can wrap my headdress around my nose as a makeshift face mask.

Shamed by my immediate repulsion, I held up a hand and asked, firmly but *nicely,* "Don't crowd me."

The lepers ceased moaning and one of them said, "Okay."

Okay. He didn't really say 'Okay' because that word didn't exist at this time, but he moaned something that sounded like 'Aye' and the colony slowly hobbled away, giving me six feet of space.

"What can I do for you?" I ask.

"Help us!"

"Heal us!"

"Clean us."

I shake my head, my eyes misting with tears. I give the lepers a thumbs up. "I've got you."

One month later, Guinevere is pointing to the same leper caves. I'm shocked by the transformation. What were once dank and uninviting hovels have been transformed to quaint cave-cottages that remind me of Hobbit houses. The limestone is polished to a shine. There's built-in sconces for torches, a community garden, a goat pen, and nice doors with gleaming green paint.

My public works commission has cleaned up the mess, installed a sewage system, and constructed a walkway with a handicap rail (we can't have any more lepers falling off a cliff. It's become a health hazard).

"Arthur!" Guinevere commands. "Bring the children."

Arthur and Mordred are part of Guinevere's task force. I figured they needed something to keep them busy and out of jail. They've become fast friends and faster drinking buddies (Mordred is a bad influence!). You know what they say? Idle hands breed disorderly conduct and public urination...

So I gave them jobs. Total nepotism, but I feel bad about taking Arthur's throne and leaving him unemployed.

Arthur and Mordred appear moments later, leading a group of ten children. They look like sober (thank God) Peace Corps volunteers. Arthur is holding the hand of a little boy while Mordred has a girl on his shoulders.

Guinevere kneels down and speaks softly to a little girl of about six. The girl stares up at me shyly. Her face is squeaky clean and while she's on the thin side, she seems to be gaining some weight.

"Eleanor would like to thank you for saving her nose," Guinevere says, nudging the girl gently behind the back.

Eleanor approaches me with a bouquet of daisies grasps in a hand with only three fingers. "Bless you, Queen Laurel."

"Ready?" Guinevere claps her hands and addresses the children. "Like we practiced: Hip Hip..."

Little hands reach for the sky. "Huzzah!"

"Huzzah!"

"Huzzah!"

When all the cheering ends and we mosey over to the community garden to pet the goats, Mordred pulls me aside. "You are *killing* it as queen!"

There is a time to be humble, and there's a time to own it. Today I choose to own it. "Yeah, I am!"

## 38

RUNNING a kingdom is not all about saving children and picking out tapestries. Sometimes you have to face a number of distasteful tasks.

"How many do we have to flog today?"

"Seven men, Your Majesty," Young Merlin says.

"And what is their crime?"

He reads from the scrolls. "Thievery. Public drunkenness. Inappropriate behavior with a goat. In the case of this one fellow," he peers down at the charges, "all three."

I'm perched on my throne, my legs tucked beneath me. My butt cushion is fluffier, and I've learned to make myself more comfortable in this time where comfort does not exist.

But that doesn't account for my headache. *Thinking.* Who knew being a queen requires so much thinking? It's not a hard job, but these bureaucrats make ruling harder than it needs to be.

I turn to my legal counsel. "Vicky? What say you?"

She shrugs. "Don't ask me. I'm a divorce lawyer."

"What did I hire you for? You're supposed to think so I don't have to."

Vicky shrugs. "You didn't hire me. I hired myself."

"Well, fire yourself!"

"I'm going to give myself a warning," she says. "I think I just need proper direction."

Damn it. Now I have to contemplate. After three steins of mead last night, I was hoping to phone it in this morning.

I steeple my fingers. "Young Merlin?"

"Aye?"

"Is being shitfaced not the cause of the man's thievery of the goat, thereby leading to getting familiar with said goat?"

Young Merlin's brows furrow in great contemplation. "It is possible."

"Then the solution is clear: order the pub owners of the land to water down the ale after a customer has had more than three drinks. No flogging. Waste of resources. Slap him with a fine of three bushels of wheat and six months community service at the leper colony."

"But Your Majesty!"

I rub my brow. *"What?!"*

"The kingdom enjoys a day of public shaming."

I arch an eyebrow. "That's disturbing. Who amongst the seven criminals is the worst offender?"

"This man has multiple counts of urination on church property. On the cathedral door. In the holy water. In the confessional. On the priest."

"Drunk?" I ask.

"No..."

"What an asshole," I mutter. "Okay, take him to the village square and have four men with full bladders treat him like a urinal."

Young Merlin nods, impressed. "Her Majesty is full of wise answers!"

"That's what I do." I scope the court. "Where is OG Merlin?"

"In the dungeon, Your Majesty."

"What is he doing there?"

"Visiting Morgaine le Fey," he says. "Her day of public shaming is this Sunday, as per your Magna Carta."

Vicky and I exchanged a concerned glance. As Camelot's most dangerous criminal, Morgaine is cooling her heels in solitary confinement. I've been so busy improving lives and saving children that I haven't had time to pop down and visit her. Actually, I don't want to visit her. She's like that toxic friend that drains all your energy whenever you get together, so it's better to just stuff her in the dungeon and forget about her.

Also, I don't know how I feel about Merlin visiting Morgaine. It's weird, considering they had amazing sex and I *know* Merlin was into it ... until he discovered who he was actually having sex with. What if Merlin got a taste for Morgaine and he's down there boning her right now? I object to him turning my royal dungeon into a sex dungeon!

"Is he torturing her?" I ask.

"No."

I notice the shift in Young Merlin's eyes. "What would you do?"

"I would taunt her."

"With words?"

"Perhaps," he says. "And a little light flogging."

"Sounds kinky," Vicky says.

I stand up. "Take me to the dungeons!"

39

THE DUNGEON IS LOCATED in the bowels of the castle. Accompanied by Young Merlin and Vicky, I descend a slimy staircase that spirals around and around a cold stone wall. The air is cold and clammy. Flickering torches light our way down. The stairs crumble underfoot and never seem to end.

"I didn't know the dungeons were this deep," I say, peering down into the dark abyss.

At the bottom, a guard who looks like the Grim Reaper guides us to a boat. He grins at me with a mouthful of rotten teeth. "Your Majesty."

I stop on the banks and peer at the water. "Wait! There's a river down here? I have my own river?!"

Vicky presses her clove-filled handkerchief to her nose. "It smells like a sewer."

"It is a sewer," Young Merlin says. "All the waste from the water closet collects down here."

I fight the urge to puke. "Gross!"

Vicky turns white. "I just remembered I have some scrolls I have to sign off on before the Day of Public Shaming."

"But you're a divorce lawyer!"

"And some couples are getting divorced..."

*"You're leaving me?"*

She slowly backs away. "Raincheck?"

"Take note," I call to her, "Send the public sanitation task force down here ASAP. We can't live in a castle with an open sewer line in the basement."

Vicky gives me a thumbs up.

I turn to Young Merlin. "What about you? You suddenly remember something you have to do too?"

He fixes me with a stare so foxy that I make the mistake of sucking in my breath. I inhale of lungful of nasty fumes.

Young Merlin thumps me on the back as I choke and gag. "I will remain by Your Majesty's side."

"The smell does not bother you?" I ask, wiping the tears from my eyes.

"I have a remedy for that." He taps my nose three times. The stench of sewage gives way to fresh sunshine and flowers.

"You're telling me that's what you've been smelling all this time?"

The foxy stare is made all the more tempting by a foxy smile. "My scent of choice," he whispers into my ear, "is the scent of Your Majesty's hair."

Out of the corner of my eye, I see the guard roll his eyes.

I don't know what to think. Young Merlin is super cheesy *and* super effective. I don't recall OG Merlin being this thirsty.

I arch an eyebrow. "Why are you so much more charming than your older self?"

"I, too, am disappointed with my ancient self." Young Merlin offers me a hand and guides me into the boat. "As Your Majesty would say, 'I suck.'"

We have a laugh because truly, OG Merlin does suck. I don't know what I was doing messing around with that cynical bastard when you could be with the same person, except younger, hotter, and more fun.

Such dating options weigh heavily on my mind as the guard unlocks Morgaine's cell.

We enter to the CRACK of a whip.

I'm greeted by the sight of Morgaine le Fey strung up by her wrists. She's stripped to her clammy shift. Neon blue rope binds her wrists in place of chains.

Just as I'm about to step forward and spin her around to face me, the CRACK resounds and her backs arches like a bow.

CRACK! Morgaine grits her teeth. Her body flinches.

Where's the whip? I whirl around.

OG Merlin is propped on a stool in the corner, his arms tucked into his armpits, his intense gaze pinned on Morgaine.

CRACK!

Morgaine bends and writhes like she's a tormented modern dancer.

"Merlin!" I rush forward. "What are you doing to her?"

"I am hex-whipping her."

"Stop it! It looks like torture."

"It *is* torture," Merlin says.

"Yeah, but *why*?"

I've answered my own question. Morgaine is a master of stirring up anger. A moment in her presence is enough to turn a saint into a killer.

"She will infuriate me no more!" Merlin says.

CRACK!

"ARGH," Morgaine says.

Young Merlin pokes his head inside. "Ah, hex whipping. My favorite method of torture. There was a time when I was partial to hot oil, but this is much cleaner. Well done, Merlin."

"Thank you, Merlin," says Merlin.

How can the Merlins be so blasé about wizard whipping someone to death?

"Well, stop it! You're going to kill her."

"Nothing will kill le Fey. Do you want a turn?"

"No!"

"It's very enjoyable. Remember, this is what she did to you."

Tempting...

"No! I want no part in this. I'm not the torturing kind."

"I'd like a try." Young Merlin steps forward. He aims his hands at Morgaine and her head snaps back. She grits her teeth while her body spasms out.

"Merlins! Drop her! I command it."

The two Merlins glare at me. With a sigh, OG Merlin tears his gaze away from Morgaine. The neon ropes vanish. Morgaine collapses to the floor.

"Everyone out. I'd like a word with Morgaine... *alone*."

The Merlins hesitate.

"Not a good idea, Laurel, ah, Your Majesty," OG Merlin says."Le Fey is a viper."

"I can handle her," I say, shooing them from the cell.

They linger, hovering around me like body guards. Young Merlin plants himself by the door. "Maybe we should—"

"Get out!"

Alone, I tap my foot impatiently and study Morgaine's tangled hair. I shake my head. What a pathetic sight. Despite all the wrong she's done me (the list is long), I can't help feeling sorry for the sniveling figure on the floor.

"Get up."

At last, Morgaine rises to her bare feet. She tips her head back and glares at me over the tip of her nose, her chest rising and falling from her hex-whipping.

"Morgaine." I look her up and down. "You *actually* look good."

"You sound disappointed."

"Well, yeah! You've been locked in a smelly dungeon for two months. Why do you still look so good?"

Her lips curl into a secretive smile. "Laurel," she nods, "or shall I say: *Your Majesty*."

"That's it? You're not going to thank me for saving you from an afternoon of uncomfortable wizard torture?"

"Oh, that?" She rotates her shoulders and stretches. "It's nothing more than a high intensity spanking. I rather enjoy it. *Shhh.* Don't tell Merlin or else he'll stop."

My hands furl into fists. She's more of a deviant than I thought. This is supposed to be a regular, run-of-the-mill torture dungeon, and she's managed to turn it into a BDSM dungeon. I hate and admire how she always manages to flip the situation and land on top.

"Sweeping up the serf dwellings, curing leprosy, charming Saxons..." Morgaine eyes me with admiration and dare I say it? Pride? "I heard you're killing it as queen, as I always knew you would."

I narrow my eyes. "Who told you this?"

"Mordred visits me from time to time." She steps back and takes in my red velvet gown trimmed with white fox fur. "He also told me he's working for your 'Cure Leprosy' task force... alongside Arthur?"

"Yup."

"You found Mordred gainful employment?" She arches a doubtful brow. "And he likes it?"

"I think he likes it. He hasn't missed a day of work."

Morgaine claps. "Once again, I'm right. You are a better queen than I've predicted. All our strife could have been cut short if you'd just done what I told you to do."

"Are you trying to butter me up to get out of jail?"

Morgaine bats her lashes. "Maybe."

I roll my eyes. "What more do you want, Morgaine? You've already got your wish. I'm Queen of the Britons. Arthur has an ordinary job at the leper colony. Destiny fulfilled."

She squares her shoulders. "I shall take your place once you return to your time."

"That's it? That's your master plan?"

"Yup."

The nerve! "Who says I want to return to my time? I'm thriving here. *My* people are thriving because of me and I've got plans to... build a highway *and* a dam."

Morgaine gathers her hair from her face. "Have you checked your Instagram?"

I suck in my breath. It's an innocent enough question, but it takes me for a spin. "I haven't had time. I've been pretty busy."

"Check your Instagram."

I yank out my phone and pull up my account for the first time in two months. "This can't be right... "

I take a step back, fumbling for support, shooketh to my core. "Why is... what the... what the fucccccccccck?"

40

I'M IMAGINING THINGS. "1.2 Million followers?!"

Morgaine looks like the cat that got the cream. "Pleased?"

"But I haven't posted anything since ... Universal Studios."

I flip through my feed. There's a picture of me in my favorite blood-red velvet dress with white minx trim set against a green hedgerow. My hair is pulled back in Medieval princess braids and accessorized with holly. Vivid colors. Excellent composition and depth of field. Maximum Christmas vibes. That picture gets 60.4K Likes.

There's a candid of me showing the shit shovelers how to shovel shit, which doesn't sound like the most glamorous subject for a photo op, but trust me, I look both epic and relatable.

More photos follow. I'm holding a little girl in my arms while the leper children gaze up at me with adoring faces. My hair is wrapped in a blue scarf and I resemble the ultimate stylish humanitarian relief worker. I'm Princess Diana 2.0. I remember this day, but I don't remember anyone snapping my photo.

"Where did these pictures come from?"

"Mordred," Morgaine says. "Still wants his mother's approval, so he did a little favor for me." She studies my face as I study my photos. "Do you like them?"

"Like them? I freaking love them!"

How did I end up choosing Merlin, who doesn't give a fuck if his thumb is in the frame to be my Instagram Boyfriend? I'm hiring Mordred from now on.

I shake my head, overwhelmed by so many conflicting emotions. Morgaine's hacked into my account and blackmailed me before. She's posted Merlin's god awful photos of me, which should have never seen the light of day and made me lose a grip of followers, including my brand deal with Ainsley Mills.

Already I see messages pop up in my DM. A quick check of my inbox yields tempting subject lines from bigger, better brands reaching out for a collaboration.

Morgaine was poison for my social media presence. Now she's repairing the damage and then some. Only question is...

"Why?" I ask. "Why help me?"

"It was part of our bargain."

"Which bargain? There's been so many." And frankly, I zone out 80% of everything Morgaine says. I should really start paying attention. There's useful information in there!

Morgaine rolls her eyes. "The one prior to the soul swap."

"Ah yes."

"You don't remember, do you?"

"Of course I do!"

She shakes her head. "The deal was you help me take Arthur's throne and I help you build your social media clout. You take the throne. I give you the followers."

"That's awesome! Thanks, Morgaine!"

She taps her foot. "Now is there something you want to give me?"

I frown. Where is she going with this? "You want out of jail?"

"That's part of it." She holds out her hands and wiggles her slender fingers. "Camelot. Give it to me."

"*Give* it to *you*? But *I'm* queen."

"And you've done a fine job," Morgaine say. "Now you don't have to worry your pretty little head over ruling a kingdom anymore. I'll take over from here and you can return home and resume 'influencing.'"

I narrow my eyes. I see where she's going with this. All her talk about Operation Royal Takeover and how I'll be a much better ruler than Arthur was pure and utter bullshit.

The crown was never intended for me. She wanted me to do her dirty work while she swoops in and takes all the credit. And the throne.

Not. On. My. Watch.

"Actually," I say, pocketing my phone, "I'm good."

"What do you mean?"

"I'm good as queen," I say. "I've got plenty of influence in Camelot and I'm pretty comfortable here, so... I'm going to keep on keepin' on."

Morgaine steps toward me. Her eyes gleam murder and she's reaching for me like she wants to strangle me. Seriously. Morgaine is so easy to read.

I dodge her advance and back toward the door.

"We are not finished," she says. "The throne is mine! Camelot is mine!"

"Yeah, except," I challenge with a carefree shrug, "I'm queen and you're a prisoner in *my* kingdom."

The door opens and my two Merlins flank the entryway, ready to crack their hex-whips in case Morgaine tries to jump me.

Morgaine grits her teeth. Her tangled black hair curtains a face that hadn't seen sunlight in two months. With her dirty white shift, bare feet, and homicidal expression, she looks like the girl from *The Ring*. She points a finger at me and spits. "You will *rue* the day you betrayed me."

"I'm sure I will," I say, and try to think of a badass retort. "But first, *you* will rue the many times you tried to kill me."

I jump as a blast of purple lightning obliterates the stone wall inches from my head.

I signal the Merlins. They nod and roll up their sleeves.

"Don't spare the hex-whip, boys."

The dungeon cell blaze with blue wizard light. In seconds, Morgaine's lethal hands are detained in magic rope.

I halt halfway out the door. "Oh, and Morgaine? Tomorrow is the day of public shaming. I was going to pardon you, but because you're such an unredeemable asshole, I think..." My lips twist into a vindictive smile. "... I'm about to get Medieval on your sorceress ass."

## 41

THAT EVENING I treat myself to a steaming hot bubble bath and a mud mask.

Two servants were tasked with carting buckets of hot water up three flights of stairs to fill the tub. It took five trips from the kitchens to the royal bedchambers. By the time they were finished, they were huffing and puffing and sweating bullets. One page boy looked like he was about to bust a vein. They probably don't know it, but this is great weight training. A year of this and they'll be ready to train as knights.

I give each page boy a pouch of gold coin.

"Is this all for us?" Page Boy 1 asks.

"Yup."

"Oh thank you, Your Majesty! Thank you!"

They bless me and tell me I'm the best master and queen they've ever had. I do not doubt it. I'm starting to think I'm the best monarch England has ever seen.

I wave off their excessive groveling. I have one more request. "Have Merlin come to my chambers."

"Which Merlin?"

My lips twitch. "*Both* Merlins..."

Alone, I dump a bottle of hotel soap from my bag (never time travel without bringing your own soap) and sink into the tub.

The warm water relaxes my muscles. My muscles are not particularly sore. I didn't do anything strenuous, but seeing Morgaine hex-whipped gave me phantom neck cramps. I scrub the dungeon funk from my body with lavender scented soap. I have a goblet of red wine within arm's reach, my luxurious royal bathrobe laid out on my bed, and a fire flickering in the hearth. A quick check of my Instagram boasts 23K new followers, cementing my meteoric rise in social media stardom. Things are good. Things are finally coming up Laurel.

A knock at my door.

I raise my goblet. "Come in."

The two Merlins poke their heads inside. They see me submerged in my bubble bath and hesitate at the entrance.

"Close the door behind you," I say, checking them out. They are washed and cleaned and dressed in matching navy robes with gold trim.

Young Merlin takes one look at my soapy naked shoulders and turns red.

OG Merlin is instantly suspicious. He eyes the bear rug by the fire and the extra goblets by the decanter. His lips twitch. "You summoned us, Laurel, er... Your Majesty."

"Indeed." I flick a soap sud from my arm. "I need Merlin to scrub my back."

OG Merlin clears his throat. "Which Merlin?"

"I choose you."

Young Merlin looks to OG Merlin with envy. "You're a lucky man."

I kick up my leg and wiggle my toes. "You can rub my feet."

"Don't you have ladies to attend to your bathing needs?" OG Merlin asks.

I hold out the sponge and Young Merlin eagerly scurries to take it. "I gave them the night off."

OG Merlin lingers by the door. "You'll need someone to dry you off."

I meet his eye. "I was hoping you can both help me with that."

"Both of us?" He arches an eyebrow. "Shall we take turns?"

"It's more efficient if you work as a team."

He tries to hide his smile. "Is that a royal order?"

I slump back in my tub and stretch out my arms. Water sloshes over the side and the bubbles shift, giving the wizards a good look at my assets.

Young Merlin drops the sponge. OG Merlin rolls up his sleeves. He dips his hands in the bathwater and *ooooh. Hello.*

"You missed my foot."

OG Merlin pins me with his sinister, sexy stare. "I know."

I loll my head back. "It's good to be queen."

42

I OVERSLEEP my alarm and arrive late to the Day of Public Shaming.

"Sorry. Sorry. Coming through." I step over someone's foot and squeeze my way to my throne (not my actual throne, but a bougie travel one made of wicker and sporting the same pompous high back design).

Vicky is seated to my right, also in a high-back chair but not as fancy as my wicker throne. Her hair is done up into a crazy double bun held together by twenty braids, and she's wearing a green gown with thorns embroidered on the skirt. Total evil Disney villainess outfit.

I'm in a blue gown with fluted sleeves (this must be the fashion this season) and a wicked cool gold braided corset. I didn't have time to do my hair or makeup. The sun is bright and glaring, causing me to reach for my sunglasses only to remember I forgot them in the future.

"I am so so sooooo sorry," I say, massaging my sore head. I wish the castle had a Starbucks or even bad diner coffee. "The ceremony hasn't started yet, has it?"

"You're the queen," Vicky says. "The ceremony can't start unless you're here."

Vicky gives me a critical side-eye. "Late night partying?"

I shift in my seat. "One can say that."

"You look hungover."

"I am," I say with a sheepish grin. "I had two bottles of wine."

She sniffs. "Thanks for the invite."

"It was a private party..."

I tap my fingers on my armrest, waiting for Vicky to ask me about it. "A *very* private party," I continue, "*if you know what I mean.*"

"Uh huh." Vicky's surreptitiously browsing her phone. Fluted sleeves are great for hiding phones so a random serf doesn't spot it and cry 'witch.'

"We are almost out of portable chargers," she mumbles. "How are we going to charge our phones now?"

"Merlin knows a way."

"How?"

"He harnesses lightning like Benjamin Franklin and directs it into some orbs and shit."

Vick pokes her head up. "Cool."

"That Merlin..." I sigh. "He's great with his hands."

"Uh huh." Vicky is totally disinterested.

"Young Merlin, too. They work well as a team."

"I'm sure they do," she says, attention still pinned on her phone. "Given they are the same person separated by two years." Finally, she looks up and notices the empty seats. "They're late, too."

"Oh, they're recovering."

"Recovering from what?"

I summon a page boy for my morning mead. "The party."

Vicky narrows her eyes and takes in my disheveled hair and stupid grin. *"No..."*

I nod. "Oh yeah."

Her eyes widen. "You didn't!"

"I did."

Vicky glances around our platform seats. "Both of them?" she lowers her voice. "At the same time?"

"On a bear rug. In front of a fire. It's like everything you could ask for in your Medieval sex dream."

"I've never had any Medieval sex dreams. Laurel, you hoe... I don't wanna know!" She glances around again. "What was it like?"

"They coordinate superbly, almost like they have one mind."

"They *do* have one mind."

"Overall, I'd rate the experience an 8.5."

"Not a ten? Your first threesome?!"

"Technically, it's not a threesome. I slept with the same guy, just two versions of him."

"But were there two dicks?"

Heat floods my body from head to toe. I clear my throat. "Oh yeah."

"That's a threesome," Vicky says.

"That's part of the problem. I never dreamed I'd be so busy!"

Vicky frowns. "Meaning?"

"There's a lot of multi-tasking involved," I say. "It reminds me of the latex company where I had to answer the phone, compose an email while taking the office Starbucks order, and fix the fax machine."

Vicky blinks. "Your office still has a fax machine?"

"I know, right? The owner is stuck in his ways."

She motions for me to get to the point. "So threesome?"

"Right. Loads of multitasking, then attrition. Your legs tire and your mouth... and your mind wanders to other things."

"What kind of things?"

"Like if we're going to make a mess on the bear rug. It's a newly skinned bear, a gift from the Saxons, and I don't think they'd appreciate it if we ruin it the first day. There's no dry cleaning in Camelot."

Vicky shakes her head in disappointment. "Only you would complain about working too hard in a threesome with two wizards."

We watch the courtier seats fill up with brightly dressed nobles. The peasants amass on both sides of the muddy road.

"This is a strange conversation," I mouth.

"Just a drop of water in an ocean of strange events," Vicky says.

We glance over our shoulders as the Merlins join us on the VIP platform.

"Your Majesty." They wink in unison.

Blushing, I wink back. "Merlins."

Nudging me in the ribs, Vicky whispers in my ear. "Did their... swords cross?"

"Sometimes," I whisper back, "but because they're the same person, it's like the two swords joined into one... mighty sword."

Vicky glances back at the Hot Merlins. "Damn. I want to know what it's like to sleep with a wizard."

"You slept with Morgaine. And now we're going to publicly shame her. Speaking of which..."

I scope out the attendance and take a mental roll call. Arthur. Gwen. Lancelot. The knights. Percival and that husky dude who wears his armor backwards. All the serfs. The fishmonger and the stable master. Two Merlins. Vicky. A stylish queen in the bluest dress of the land and cute elvish slippers (it's me!).

Mordred is the only one absent, which is understandable. I wouldn't want to attend the public humiliation of my mother either. Mordred hates his mother, but it's still hard to watch. He's going to need intensive therapy, the poor little shit.

The trumpeters herald the beginning of the festivities. An ox cart carrying the prisoners trundle down the bumpy road. The spectators curse and jeer, chucking rotten vegetables at the criminals. Whereas the other prisoners huddle in fear, Morgaine stands like a martyr with her hands bound behind her. A tomato *splats* her white shift. She doesn't flinch or blink.

Her hair is braided, and she is as serene and beautiful as a tragic heroine.

"Who the fuck braided her hair?" I mutter to my advisors.

"I believe she did it herself," Merlin says.

"The guard has a lot to answer for. Three French braids require help. She looks great." I touch my own tangled hair. "She's going to make me look like an asshole."

"Don't worry," Vicky says. "Everyone knows *she's* the asshole."

I smooth the wrinkles from my gown. "I've never been to a public shaming. What do I do? Oh shit, am I supposed to give a speech?"

"The kingdom will want to hear from their queen," Young Merlin says.

"I didn't write one."

Vicky taps me on the shoulder. "I'm sure you'll come up with something."

I suppose I'll just have to wing it.

Right. I can handle that. My people love simple words and ideas you don't have to think much about, ergo, I'll just say whatever comes to mind.

"What happens at a public shaming, exactly? What's on the itinerary?"

"Whatever you desire," OG Merlin reminds me. "The executioners are waiting for your command."

"Executioners?" I peer at the platform and spot a muscular hulk of a man in a black hood presiding over a table of nasty torture instruments. "You never said anything about execution."

"What did Your Majesty think will happen?"

All I know of public shaming involves people being dragged through the Twitter coals. "I thought we'd march them through the streets and roast them."

Merlin's eyes light up with sadistic glee. "We can roast them."

"Not that kind of roasting." I rub my temple. "Vicky... explain."

"We'll call them nasty names until they apologize for being assholes and then we criticize their apologies."

"That will not entertain the kingdom," OG Merlin says. "Some prisoners will be executed. *All* will be shamed before your subjects. How will Your Majesty like to proceed?"

He catches my blank expression and hands me a scroll — a list of names with corresponding crimes and punishments.

"Gross." I poke my head up, "Do you really need to maim this cattle thief?"

"What would Your Majesty suggest?" Both Merlins ask.

"A fine of two cows would suffice." I scan the list. "Dairy farm arson resulting in the death of three. Oh man... hang this one. Highway robber—injuries, but no deaths. I don't think he needs to be tortured. A light flogging should cover it, no execution. Put him on three years communal toilet clean up with probation on good behavior."

"The queen is just," Young Merlin says, scribbling away with his quill.

At last I come to Morgaine's crime: Treason. Unlawful witchcraft. Attempted assassination. Incest. Vandalism of royal property. Tax evasion.

Vicky reads over my shoulder, "That doesn't even cover half the crimes she's committed in other centuries."

"Not to mention the many times she's tried to kill me," I say. "But don't you think drawing and quartering her sounds a bit harsh?" I turn to Vicky. "Didn't they do that to Mel Gibson in *Braveheart*?"

"Is *that* what the executioner was doing? I thought they were jiggling his balls."

"No. I'm pretty sure they were gutting him with a dull knife and yanking out his entrails."

Vicky grimaces. "That's barbaric."

"And unsanitary..." I shiver. "Yeah, no. We're not doing that."

Both Merlins blink. A silent message passes between OG Merlin and his younger self. *Should you tell her or should I?*

"But the people love the sight of entrails. It's tradition: the jesters toss the innards into the crowd. People grab them as keepsakes. It's a sign of luck if you grab the stomach. Or the heart," Young Merlin says. "And blood. A healthy pool of blood marks the beginnings of the day's merrymaking."

*Yikes!*

Okay. Mordred is not alone. *Everyone* in Camelot needs therapy. I need to hire a shrink for the kingdom. ASAP. "Not on my watch."

Merlin folds his arms across his chest. "How will you punish her instead?"

I toss him the scroll. "I have a few ideas."

43

CAN I BE HONEST? I have no ideas.

All I know is if I see someone wearing Morgaine's intestines by the end of the day, I'm going to puke. What the fuck is wrong with these people?

I stand up and grip the railing of my VIP box.

The rowdy crowd doesn't appear to notice that their queen is ready to speak. I nod to Merlin. He signals the trumpeters and they bellow a jaunty tune. The spectators hush up; all heads turn to me.

I clear my throat. "Hey everyone. Welcome to my Day of Public Shaming. This is quite the turn out..."

My mind draws a blank.

Oh shit. I'm too hungover to bullshit. And I still have *no idea* what I plan to do with Morgaine. I need to stall.

"This is painful," Vicky mumbles.

I shoot her a dirty look and take a deep breath. "LET'S DO THIS!"

A cheer erupts throughout the kingdom. Serfs pump their fists, huzzah-ing and dumping lukewarm mead over each other's heads. The energy is as vicious and bloodthirsty as a football game.

Vicky frowns at me. "Graceful, Laurel. Very graceful. Are we at a wrestling match?"

"It works... move aside, bitch. I'm on a roll."

I motion for the guards to unload the criminals and line them up in front of me.

Morgaine is the last to descend. She gazes up at me, impressed and a little confused by the direction I'm taking with this.

I raise my hands and feed off the energy. "What a bunch of assholes! How about we do a little shaming?"

The spectators go wild. "Shame!"

"Shame!"

"Shame!"

I point to the prisoners, jabbing my finger at Morgaine specifically. "You make me sick."

To the farm arsonist. "You're getting shamed."

To the highway robber. "You're getting shamed."

To the murderer. "You're getting shamed."

To Morgaine le Fey. "And *you*. Especially you. I've saving the biggest shaming for you."

Morgaine's smoky eyes shimmer. *Bring it.*

"Guards! Get these losers out of my sight."

The head guard shoves the first criminal into the street. He falls to his knees and struggles to stand as people sling rotten vegetables, mud, pebbles, and God knows what filth at him.

"Shame!"

The next man is pushed, kicking and screaming, after the first and he's immediately subjected to mud slinging and name calling. The guards march the criminals through the streets and shove them into a gauntlet of shame.

These serfs are experts at trash talking and trolling. Vicky and I share a nervous look. We're both shook by the vitriol of the kingdom. Some things they're saying are vicious and downright mean. I cringe as the younger of the criminals (a petty cattle thief of no more than thirteen) bursts into tears. I would too if someone said that about my face.

Not only are the criminals complete assholes, but my entire kingdom are full of assholes. I mean, you have to be an asshole to trash talk to that degree.

And then it occurred to me...

*I'm* the queen who encouraged these assholes to be assholes...

What does that make me? I'm the one who wrote 'don't be an asshole' in my Magna Carta, and I can't even follow my own advice.

I'm having a change of heart. I can't stand by and watch these shitty people be bullied by the entire kingdom, no matter how much they deserve it.

As the prisoners slog toward the torture platform, I shoot a cautious glance at the executioner. He must be seven feet tall if he was a foot, a hulking giant with a tight ass. He's shirtless (I could have sworn he was wearing a tunic but he must've stripped for the job) and every inch of his impressive torso is packed with muscle.

I poke Vicky in the ribs. "Are you seeing what I'm seeing?"

Vicky narrows her eyes. "The executioner's six pack?"

"Is it me or is he kind of hot?"

She fans herself. "I've yet to find the castle gym. Why are all these guys so stacked?"

"Must be something in the mead," I say. "Wish we can see his face. He could be a real dog."

"Who cares about his face," Vicky says, checking out his low-slung leather pants. "With hip dips like that, he can keep the mask on. He has big dick energy."

The executioner is sharpening his ax while his scrawny assistants are polishing old blood off a very big hook. It takes me a while to peel my eyes away from the executioner's biceps.

"Young Merlin," I whisper. "What's the hook for?"

"For stringing the condemned up by the entrails."

My face turns white. Again with the entrails! "I'm thinking of putting a stop to this. We've had enough shaming for one day."

Both Merlins regard me like I've lost my mind.

"That will not be possible," OG Merlin says. "The people want justice."

"They want blood is what they want. We've got a situation here. I rule over a kingdom of hungry wolves."

"Then feed them," Young Merlin says.

"I don't want to feed them! I want to stop them." I raise my arms to give another speech. "Atten — "

OG Merlin loops an arm around my waist and drags me out of sight. "You do *not* want to do that," he says, setting me down on my feet.

I glare at him. "I can do whatever I want. I'm queen!"

He sighs. "The wolves have tasted blood. You've promised them a day of public shaming. You cannot take it back."

"Sure I can. What's the worst that can happen?"

"They will turn on you."

My eyes widen. "No way! I'm the queen."

He shakes his head. "The monarchy is an unstable symbol. Lose the trust of your people, lose your head."

"After all I've done for them?!"

"People have short memories. They only remember the last thing you did and you want to take away their fun."

"I want to ask them to be humane. To be excellent to each other."

Merlin levels me with a warning glare. "They will not be happy."

I'm well acquainted with how quickly a mob can turn against you, but I can't fathom how my kingdom can turn against me over something as stupid as their queen ordering them to be nice.

Actually...

Now that I think about it...

Asking assholes not to be assholes is probably the most dangerous thing a person can do.

"Shit." I sigh in defeat. Okay. Unless I want to run the shame gauntlet, I can't stop the mob, and I *definitely* don't want to stick around once the executioner gets his hands on the prisoners. Also, being queen sucks. I've been sold a bill of goods. I thought I had absolute power. Now I learn that I can be toppled if I don't tell the kingdom what they want to hear. Well... fuck that.

I strip off my crown and toss it to Merlin. "I'm out."

44

VICKY and the two Merlins crowd around me. "You're quitting?!"

"Yup." I roll up my sleeves and reach for my phone. "It's been real, but this queen thing is not fun anymore and my subjects are assholes. I'm out. Vicky? You coming?"

"Where are we going?" Vicky asks.

"Back home to my 1.2 million followers..." Okay. Sorry. That was a humble brag. Can't help it. The truth of the matter is, I have a lot going on for me in my time (thanks Morgaine). Why waste my life twiddling my thumbs on the throne when I can be modeling cute outfits and raking in brand sponsorship money?

Vicky contemplates the new plans for all of a second. "As much as I like being a parliament member," she says, "I miss the L.A. food scene."

"Omigod, I can totally go for some kimchi tacos right now."

"Bacon wrapped hotdogs outside the Staples Center!"

Vicky's sighs with longing. "The sushi boxes at Sugarfish."

"And good ole Korean BBQ night followed by boba runs."

My stomach growls. Despite all the lavish banquets I've sat through, the cuisine in Camelot is pretty bland. Nothing is spiced right or spiced at all.

"Okay," Vicky slaps her hands together. "How are we doing this? Are you going to abdicate after the execution?"

"I'm not staying for the executions. I'm peacin' out right now." I turn to the Merlins. Regret weighs me down. "I don't suppose either of you want to come back with us? I know you have your 'duty' to the kingdom and 'loyalty' to the crown. Oh, shit... I suppose I should put Excalibur back in the stone."

"What shall we do in this 'future'?" Young Merlin asks.

"Whatever you want," I say.

OG Merlin rains on his own parade. "There isn't a high demand for wizards."

"Or you don't have to do anything," I tell Young Merlin. I figure if OG Merlin is hell bent on staying in Camelot and being miserable, I can at least talk his younger self into tagging along. Either way, I'll have a Merlin and it won't even be considered settling because he's the same guy. "Just go with the flow. Figure it out as you go along. Lord knows I do. Are you in?"

"I am intrigued," Young Merlin says. "Where will I stay?"

"You can bunk with me." I arch an eyebrow at OG Merlin. "And you can stay here and clean up the mess. I know you love to work."

Merlin takes a long look at the vengeful crowd. "We shall return the sword to the stone and I will make sure Arthur finds it."

I sigh. "So you'll stay?"

His eyebrows shoot up. "Stay?" He takes a long look at the mud-slinging, trash-talking crowd. "Where are we eating after this?"

"Korean barbecue!"

A flicker of hesitation. "I have been unappreciated and over-worked long enough," he says, dumping his scrolls on the throne. "The time has come for the Merlin to have fun."

I'VE DECIDED against making a speech declaring my abdication. I don't want to make a big deal out of it and frankly, I'm afraid to deal with the repercussions of angering an already riled up mob. So I plan to do what any responsible monarch would do: I'm going to sneak away.

The four of us take a quick detour to the hill where I pulled Excalibur from the stone and got myself into this mess. With little fanfare, I jam Excalibur back in place and slap my hands together. "That ought to do it."

I attach a note to the sword hilt.

*DEAREST CAMELOT,*

*I quit.*

*Whoever can take the sword from the stone shall be my replacement. You know the drill. Hopefully, your new king or queen keeps my Magna Carta, particularly the 'don't be an asshole' law because ya'll need to work on that...*

*It's been real.*

*Love,*

"I THINK THAT SAYS IT ALL," I say, reading the note over.

Vicky and the Merlins triangulate a covert look. Ever get the feeling your friends are talking about you behind your back?

"Very eloquent, Your Majesty." Young Merlin's eyes shift sideways.

"Call me Laurel."

"Okay, Laurel," Vicky clasps me on the shoulder, "let's ditch this popsicle stand."

"My thoughts exactly."

My second trip to Camelot has been *way* more pleasant than my first, but as Dorothy says, there's no place like home. Home is infinitely more appealing when you have 1.2 million Instagram followers like I do. Not a brag. Just facts.

I hold out my phone and input the date and location. Everyone huddles. "We're good? Oven turned off? Everything squared away?"

Vicky gives me a thumbs up.

The Merlins nod.

And then, out of morbid curiosity and against our better judgement, we check out the executioner's stage.

From our vantage point on the hill, we have an unobstructed view of the proceedings. We missed quite a lot during our time out, but it looks like the executioner is getting shit done.

The dairy farm arsonist is dangling from a noose. There's a pool of blood against the flogging post, and the executioner's assistants are in the process of tying Morgaine down. One man works her hands, stretching them over her head. The other man tightens the rope around her ankles until she's spread eagle on a giant sundial. If I were in her place, I would be freaking the fuck out, but Morgaine is as calm as a sociopathic sorceress can be while waiting to be drawn and quartered before a bloodthirsty audience. You'd have to applaud her.

But stupid me...

I feel sorry for her. I know. *I know.* I never learn my lesson.

Vicky nudges me out of my reverie. "What's the hold up?"

"Do you think we ought to help her?"

Vicky and the two Merlins glare at me like I've lost my mind.

"Morgaine le Fey is a dangerous criminal," OG Merlin says. "She deserves to answer for her crimes."

"Yeah, but... look at her." I gesture to the stage. "She looks so pathetic and in moments some vicious serf is going to take her entrails back home as a souvenir! I wouldn't wish that on my worst enemy. Vicky! Back me up here."

Vicky wrinkles her nose. "This is Morgaine we're talking about here. She'll stab you in the back again. She can't help herself."

I look to the Merlins for mercy.

They shake their heads. "Morgaine doesn't deserve your kindness," OG Merlin says.

I turn to Young Merlin, the nicer of the two. "What about you? Surely you don't agree with... yourself."

Young Merlin clears his throat. "The world is better without le Fey."

Damn. Cold. They are so cold.

"I'm surprised by all of you." I survey their blank faces. "Sure Morgaine is a conniving, backstabbing biotch but that doesn't mean she doesn't deserve mercy. Remember all the fun times we've had with her? Vicky? You know what I'm talking about..."

Vicky lowers her head, blushing. "She was an excellent lover."

Not the angle I was going for here, but I'll take it. "And Merlin!" I swat OG Merlin in the ribs. "You scumbag! You know what she's talking about too."

OG Merlin's brows knit into a frown. "That's different. I thought she was you."

Young Merlin's face contorts in a mixture of disgust and curiosity. "You bedded le Fey?" he asks his older self.

OG Merlin reddens. "*She* took advantage of *me*."

I pound my fists into my palm. "Sure, Morgaine's wronged all of us, but she has some things going for her."

Vicky arches an eyebrow. "Such as?"

"Things... like..." I'm quiet for a minute. Wow. Trying to come up with a pro-list for Morgaine is more difficult than I thought. "She gave me a discount on my phone repair."

Vicky and the Merlins narrow their eyes at me.

"And... *and* she took us on a shopping spree to the Glendale Galleria! Merlin... she bought you that Orange Julius."

OG Merlin grumbles. "It was a tasty beverage."

"And Vicky..."

Vicky folds her arms across her chest.

"You got the most expensive pair of acid-washed jeans at the mall. Morgaine paid for it without batting an eye."

"So she bought me a pair of jeans. Big deal!"

"It's a sign of generosity."

"Buying me things?"

"Yeah," I say. "How else do you express generosity?"

Vicky sighs. "All right. We'll save her ass. *But* that's it. She's on her own after that."

"Totally. Operation Save Morgaine's Ass." I turn to the Merlins. "You two in?"

The Merlins grunt. "Aye... fine."

I slip my phone back in my pocket. "Let's do this."

We're halfway down the hill and preparing to sneak back to the main event when someone calls, "Room for three more?"

I check over my shoulder and blink three times to make sure I'm not imagining things.

Three guys stand behind us. They're dressed in high-top sneakers, MC Hammer pants, and shiny aluminum jackets. There's a lot of shoulder harnesses and wallet chains going on.

"Who are these characters?" Vicky murmurs. "They look like cyberpunk douchebags."

"Who do you think?" I whisper back. "Mordred?"

Her eyes widen. *"Mordred?!"*

He nods at me. "The one and only."

I narrow my eyes and study his companions. A scrawny guy with a red mohawk and aluminum wrap-around glasses. A giant dude in tiny white sunglasses.

"No way! Weasel? Brick Shithouse?! I thought you were dead!"

"They were," Mordred says.

"I saw Brick... I mean Ernest mowed down by a machine gun. Was I imagining things?" I wave to Ernest, who waves back. "And Nestor was gut shot."

OG Merlin takes a step back. "I saw the same thing." His suspicious gaze swings to Mordred. "Interesting."

"Did *you* do this?" I ask.

In reply, Mordred strips off his black leather motorcycle gloves and cracks his knuckles. Red sparks dance at his fingertips.

His henchmen yank off their sunglasses, revealing glowing red cyborg eyes.

"I told you I would never leave my friends behind," Mordred says.

I gawk at Brick Shithouse's face. The left side is a mess of bullet holes patched up with metal plates... Holy shit! Mordred's resurrected his dead friends and turned them into zombie cyborgs.

I gulp. "You never told me you were a wizard."

"You never asked," Mordred says, slipping his motorcycle glove back on.

Makes sense. Mordred *is* Morgaine's son, after all.

I peer at Weasel's glowing red eyes. Yikes! He's terrifying. I manage a weak wave. "Hey Nestor."

He waves back. "Hey."

Creepy terminator vibes aside, he still sounds like the same old Weasel.

"How do you feel about being resurrected, Ernest?"

Brick Shithouse grunts and gives me a thumbs up. Aw. He's back and still a cuddly teddy bear who can crush you like a beer can if you get on his bad side.

I check out Mordred's pants. "Is that Velcro?"

Mordred yanks on one of the straps. *Zchick.*

"Did you take a trip back to the '80s?"

*Zchick.* "My favorite decade," he says. *Zchick.*

"Fascinating." Young Merlin comes closer. "May I?"

"Have at it." Mordred holds up his hands. He turns to OG Merlin. "How about you, Uncle? I have a strap here with your name on it."

OG Merlin hesitates. "I'll just test the one..."

*Zchick. Zchick. Zchick.*

Mordred catches Vicky's eyes. "I've got a special one for you, Legs. Come and get it."

Vicky rolls her eyes. "Laurel, can we please..."

I clap my hands together. "Stop playing with Mordred's pants!"

The Merlins back away, shamed.

"Okay," I say to Mordred, "I might as well just get this out there. Have you come back to kill us?"

Mordred smooths the sides of his mohawk. "I'm a healer, not a killer. We've returned to save Mom."

I turn to Vicky. "The more the merrier, right?"

46

<hr>

The executioner approaches Morgaine with a grisly hook.

He lumbers, not because *he's* slow, but for theater's sake. The audience enjoys a drawn out torture.

He bides his time lurching about the stage and sharpening his ax, which he won't use until the very end.

Until the prisoner, devoid of her entrails (but still alive), has pled for mercy.

He'll strike her head from her body. The audience will swarm, soaking up her blood with filthy handkerchiefs as a keepsake of this day. Her head will be mounted on a pike and taken to the castle battlements as a warning to all.

After the crowds disperse to the pubs, he'll clean up the blood and gory bits and work until sundown to dismantle the stage. It's a long day and a hard job for surprisingly little pay and no respect. He still farms like everyone else. The kingdom cheers him when he's covered in blood and avoids him like a leper on his days off.

If it weren't for his father and his father's father being the royal executioner, he'd rather be doing something else. Anything else.

Royal falconer?

Royal cook? He does make a scrumptious meat pie, if he does say so himself.

The prisoner, one Morgaine le Fey, is a criminal of notoriety: treasonous sorceress, assassin, tax evader.

The last bit is understandable. The taxes in Camelot are one of the highest in the land, and even higher with the new queen and her public works projects. Rubbish, if you ask him. If the queen wants to build a communal toilet, surely she can fund it by selling her fancy fur cloaks instead of taxing the good people of Camelot.

To make matters worse, Queen Laurel is reluctant to execute her prisoners, even going as far as pardoning the lot of them. That's all fine and dandy for the criminals, but doesn't put bread on his table. After a disappointing wheat harvest, he's been known to pocket a few coins himself.

The executioner looms over the prisoner, the sharp end of his hook glistening in the sun. It's no surprise that he cuts a menacing figure. What *is* a surprise, however, is le Fey's blank reaction. By now, even the brawniest men would be in tears, but this woman barely bats an eye.

She's on her back, her arms drawn over her head, her ankles bound by ropes. Her hair spills behind her like ink and her skin is fair, pink, and soft.

A twinge of pity causes him to lower his hook. He couldn't see anything dangerous about this bonny lass, who looks more like a fairytale princess than an enemy of the queen.

Morgaine's gaze skates across his naked torso and settles on his arms, bare and bulging with muscle. Her rosy lips part in an exhale.

"You're a tall drink of water," she says, peering into his eyes and trying to discern what he looks like behind his hood. "Do you really have to do this? How about we call off this silly execution and go to the pub?"

He blinks in surprise. That was a first. He'd had prisoners cry, plead, and curse him, but no one has ever ... asked him to the pub.

Le Fey *is* a wicked woman... wickedly appealing.

He clears his throat and holds up the hook. "Sorry, ma'am. Duty calls."

Morgaine sighs. "It was worth a shot. All right, do what you must." She arches her back, causing her bosom to strain her transparent white shift. "Be gentle..."

He gulps. This is the part of the job he always hated. He stammers another apology, and she shrugs as much as her bindings would allow.

"Nothing personal," she says. "I enjoyed the way you *took care* of the other. You were efficient. I like that."

"I promise you won't suffer."

"You're about to draw and quarter me. I think I might feel a little pain."

He clears his throat. "Sorry, ma'am."

"No need to apologize. On with it."

Without meeting her eyes, he rips apart her shift with the hook, baring her to the navel. He glances down at her creamy skin and feels a pang of regret. Under different circumstances, he would have very much like to court this woman, but as fate would have it, he was destined to slice her open and cut off her head.

Stammering a third apology, he raises the hook, aiming for her chest when a shout of alarm ripples through the crowd.

An arm, almost as bulky as his own, loops around his neck, choking him. His attacker knocks the hook from his hands.

The executioner has always been the biggest man in Camelot, but today he's met his match. This fellow is equal to his size and built like a brick outhouse.

Had it not been for the executioner's own brute strength, his attacker would have crushed his windpipe. The executioner manages to squirm free, just in time to catch of glimpse of his attacker's glowing red eyes and iron-plated face.

*God's teeth! What manner of man is he?*

With a growl, the man wrestles him to the ground. He lands a kick to the man's terrifying face, but his boot has no impact. His attacker growls and crushes the executioner against his chest in a crippling bear hug.

As the executioner struggles for freedom, he notices that a strange collection of players has climbed onto his stage.

He recognizes Queen Laurel, the queen's intimidating royal advisor, and the two Merlins (odd, isn't it? He's only ever known one Merlin. One day, the kingdom learns that Merlin has a twin).

And Mordred, known to the kingdom as the son Morgaine had out of wedlock (father unknown). Mordred is dressed in a shiny metal jacket and strange balloon pants. He's joined by a scrawny fellow who looks like a human weasel.

As the big man holds him down, the weasel-man punches him in the gut and howls in pain as his fists connects with a band of rock hard muscle.

"That's enough, Nestor," Mordred says and the weasel-man whirls around, revealing a battered profile patched with iron plates.

*Who are these people?*

Queen Laurel steps forward and raises her arms. "Camelot! I revoke the death sentence of Morgaine le Fey!"

"You can't do that!" someone shouts from the crowd.

"Of course I can. I'm queen. I can totally change my mind."

A rain of rotten vegetables pelt the stage. "Boo!"

"Boo?!" Queen Laurel echoes.

"Aye! Boo!"

"Are you actually booing *me*? Your *queen*?"

A slimy apple bounces off her forehead as the tide turns.

"Kill le Fey! Kill le Fey!"

"Come on guys," Queen Laurel pleads, "don't be assholes!"

There's a murmur of misunderstanding.

*"Oi! The queen's calling us assholes!"*

*"We'll show her who's the bigger asshole."*

*"She thinks she's better than us."*

"I thought we agreed that I *am* better than you," Queen Laurel says. "That's why I'm your queen."

"Don't taunt them, Laurel," her cousin says.

"They taunted me first."

They both duck as a pumpkin sails over their heads.

The people of Camelot, deprived of their execution and taunted by their queen, bubble with anger.

*"Kill le Fey. Down with the monarchy!"*

The scary cousin whirls on the queen. "You couldn't keep your mouth shut, could you?"

Queen Laurel eyes the two Merlins and slides a finger across her throat. They nod and raise their hands.

CRACK.

Two sizzling neon blue whips snap against the platform.

"Make sure you get the flutist," Queen Laurel says. "He's the ring leader."

CRACK.

The Merlins act as a pair of lion tamers, holding back the horde as Mordred picks up the hook and slices his mother's bindings.

Morgaine rubs her wrists, her gaze fixed on the queen. "Why?"

"Because unlike you, I am *not* an asshole." Queen Laurel holds out her hand. "Truce?"

Morgaine looks to her son, to the Merlins with their magic whips, to the queen's scary advisor trading insults with a group of serfs... then at him, the executioner, currently locked in a choke-hold by the strongman.

"You did all this for *me*?" Her voice cracks.

"Don't get sappy on me now," Queen Laurel says, "The Merlins can only hold the kingdom for so long. Come with us."

After a moment of hesitation, Morgaine reaches out and clasps the queen's hands.

Queen Laurel pulls Morgaine to her feet. "Merlins! Hit them with the net!"

"I've got you," Mordred says, joining the Merlins. The trio curl their fingers into claws and trace circles in the air.

The air sizzles and snaps. The executioner blinks, unable to believe his eyes as the wizards conjure up a giant fishing net and cast it over the unruly crowd.

*"Ouch!"*

*"Cor, get this thing off me!"*

*"It's frying me hair!"*

*"It's frying me balls!"*

The executioner's jaw drops to his chest. He must be dreaming. All of Camelot is flopping around like mackerel in a magical net made of blue and red lightning. Even more fantastical still, Queen Laurel gathers everyone around a glowing brick in her hand.

"You too, Brick Shithouse... er, Ernest!" she calls. "Drop the executioner and get your ass over here!"

The big man releases his grip and the executioner fall to his knees. He's winded and gasping for breath, but at least he's not being zapped in the lightning net like the rest of the kingdom.

"Okay, everyone," says the queen. "Hands on the phone and hang on to your butts."

The executioner lifts his head to see the group place their hands on the glowing brick.

Morgaine spares him a wary glance as he struggles to his feet. "Where are we going?" she asks.

"Somewhere a lot more fun than this," Queen Laurel says. "Everyone ready?"

"Ready!"

"Here goes nothing—"

*"Wait!"* The executioner is surprised to hear himself speak.

Eight heads turn to him. He rubs his sore throat. Now that he has their attention, he's suddenly bashful.

His gaze fix on the bonny Morgaine le Fey and her eyes lock on his. "Can I come too?" he croaks.

His question stirs up a murmur of confusion.

The others glare at him with suspicion, but Morgaine's lips twitch at the corners.

She breaks from the group. "What's your name, big guy?"

He stands to his full height, causing everyone except the big man to tip their heads to the sky. "T-Thomas, ma'am."

"Please remove your hood, Thomas."

He strips off his hood. The queen and her cousin gasps. Morgaine's eyes widen, then narrow in appraisal.

"Holy shit!" Queen Laurel says. "He's hot!"

"Very, very hot," her cousin looks him up and down.

Thomas frowns. Why are they calling him 'hot'? He is actually quite chilled and wishes he had not discarded his tunic.

Morgaine props her hands on her hip. "Why do you want to leave Camelot, Thomas?"

"I am unhappy here, ma'am."

"But you're such a good executioner."

He lifts a brawny shoulder. "I am unfulfilled and the taxes are high. Please... let me come with you."

"Do you even know where we're going?"

"I don't care," he says. "So long as I don't have to lob off heads or torture anymore prisoners."

Morgaine turns to the queen.

Queen Laurel heaves a sigh. "Fine, but he's bunking with you."

"Gladly," Morgaine says, earning a grumble from the queen's cousin and Mordred.

Morgaine makes room next to her and he joins them. "Put your hands on the phone."

Thomas hesitates. He touches the 'phone' surface and is surprised by the smooth glass.

"Okay," Queen Laurel says. "Is everyone ready *now*?"

"Ready!"

Thomas turns to the beautiful woman whom he was just about to execute. "Ready," he says, meeting her eye.

Morgaine turns away with a blush.

"This may hurt a little," the queen says to him, "I hope you have a thick skull..."

Aye. That he does.

A slender hand grasps his giant one. Thomas glances down and gulps. Morgaine is holding his hand.

"Where are we going, exactly?" he asks.

"Somewhere very far away." She winks at him, causing him to sweat.

"France?"

"No," she laughs, "Not France."

Queen Laurel clears her throat. *"Ready?"*

"Sorry," Morgaine says and flashes him a private smile. "To be continued."

Rolling her eyes, the queen taps a button on her 'phone' and the world he knew, the gallows and bloody platform, dissolves into pitch blackness before a star field explodes behind his eyes.

47

---



*One year later...*

After a long wait, our group is seated at two separate tables pushed together.

The seats are small and narrow, the table top is a little sticky, and the grill at the center of each table is covered in charcoal soot. The chairs are narrow and hard on the seat. We're so crammed in that it's elbow room only. Brick Shithouse (sorry, Ernest) is probably very uncomfortable. I make a mental note to buy him a beer for being a good sport.

To this tight group in an already crowded restaurant, I ask the server to add two more chairs.

"We're expecting more people." I cast a wistful glance around the restaurant.

"They're not coming," Vicky says, after she's ordered bulgogi beef, soy garlic marinated short ribs, and pork belly for the table. "You know how she is."

"She promised she'll be here."

"Laurel... she's ghosted us all year."

"She's not very chatty."

"Hmph."

Vicky is back to working as a divorce attorney, a job that comes with no shortage of headaches. She's dating again, though she won't tell me who he or she is. I have a suspicion she's dating Brian again. Or was it Brandon? Byron? You know, the poor sap she left at the altar.

She's also started an Instagram account modeling her cute work wear outfits. In August, she's surpassed 10K followers and has become something of an influencer herself. Vicky's success doesn't come as a surprise to me. She and I share a talented Instagram boyfriend.

"Mordred," I wave to get his attention, "get a picture of Vicky and me."

Mordred, dressed in his favorite *Cobra Kai* T-shirt, snaps a photo of us on his phone.

By day, Mordred, Weasel, and Brick Shithouse attend UCLA (don't ask me how these stooges got accepted to the same school) and synchronized their chemistry classes. By night, Mordred juggles multiple side hustles (don't ask me what those are... I don't want to know), one of which is moonlighting as a lifestyle photographer. And let me tell you: his photos are — *double chef's kiss*—perfection! Mordred takes the most buttery, aesthetic photos an influencer with 1.7 million followers (and growing!) can ask for.

"Vicky," Mordred says, "relax your mouth. There you go. Laurel..." He pokes his head up from his phone and gives me a thumbs up. "Don't change a thing."

See? This is why I love Mordred. He may be a little shit, but he's proving himself to be my favorite person.

We posture for the best angles. Across the table, OG Merlin and Young Merlin roll their eyes.

"Are you two finish already?" Young Merlin asks.

OG Merlin scowls. "How many pictures is enough?"

I swear these two grumps have a hive mind.

They always agree on what show the three of us should binge on Netflix (The Crown) or what topping of pizza we order (meat lover's trio with extra cheese). I'm always outvoted two to one. Not that I'm complaining. Rooming with two Merlins has its perks.

Merlin never argues with himself, and they work as a team on everything. They're a synchronized machine when doing the dishes and doing... me. I won't get into the nitty gritty of my complicated relationship with the Merlins, but I will say that two Merlins are better than one. I feel no guilt about my harem of hot wizards because, technically, they're the same person.

In hindsight, my ill-fated trip into Le Fey's Gift & Sundry and meeting my arch nemesis worked out in the end. I was single and bitter and now I've got my hands full with two smoking hot Merlins, a closer relationship with Vicky, and a broader circle of friends including Mordred, Weasel, and Brick Shithouse, who is my *go-to* spa day friend.

I owe it all to Morgaine le Fey. She put me through hell, ruined my social media career, and tried to murder me in a variety of sick ways... Oh, and there was the time she jumped into my body and slept with Merlin. That wasn't cool.

But if she hadn't been such a pain in the ass, I wouldn't be where I am today. It's like Morgaine made me into a stronger and dare I say, *deeper* person. I'm a much more popular influencer than I was when I went to Stonehenge, and if it wasn't for Morgaine getting me fired from Ainsley Mills, I would have never sought out bigger and better brand deals. But Likes and sponsorships isn't everything (although social media clout and money is appreciated). No, a life online doesn't hold a candle to having real life friends, family, and experiences, which is why I've made it my personal goal to get the gang back together at least once a month.

As it turns out, we see each other *more* than once a month. Seriously... do they not have lives? Over the year, we've done game night, movie night, escape rooms, Friday night dinners, theme park weekends, and we're planning a Labor Day trip to San Diego in two weeks.

I've extended the olive branch to Morgaine, but she's always flaked out on me.

Our food finally comes and we dig in. Vicky takes command of the grill, frying the meats and bossing the servers around for more kimchi and pickled cucumber side dishes.

A server approaches our table. "Can we take these chairs?"

"Wait..." I glance toward the door. There's a line outside and another large group waiting to be seated and not enough chairs. My heart sinks. "I guess they're not coming after all."

I nod at the server. He takes the chairs.

With a sympathetic look, OG Merlin pours me a glass of cold beer while Young Merlin dishes a helping of spicy tofu onto my plate.

"You tried," OG Merlin says. "Le Fey is not a social creature."

"Her loss," Vicky says, taking my plate and piling it high with spare ribs and thin slices of bulgogi beef.

Shrugging off my disappointment, I dig into my plate and try to enjoy my night. I'm three lettuce wraps in when the server returns the two chairs back to our table. I drop my food when I see who's behind him.

"Morgaine! You came!" I jump up and attempt to hug her, but her pregnant belly keeps me at arm's length. "Holy shit! You look ready to pop."

"Sorry we're late. I had to pee three times before we hit the road," Morgaine says, smiling back at her fiancé.

"It's a good thing we did," Thomas the Executioner says, "there was an accident on the 405 and we were stuck for at least an hour."

"Well, we're glad you're here," I say, standing up on my tiptoe to peck Thomas on the cheek. He's almost as tall as Brick Shithouse but twice as hot.

Only Morgaine can get out of her own execution *and* hook up with the ax man. See how much better your life can be when you hook up with someone who isn't your brother? I don't know Thomas very well, but I can tell he's good for Morgaine. She's never looked so happy *and* she hasn't tried to kill me in over a year. She's even sent me a birthday gift of healing crystals and essential oils from her Malibu gift shop—and they did wonders for my insomnia.

Morgaine makes the rounds of the table, embracing Mordred and side-eyeing Vicky.

Thomas exchanges handshakes with the guys and a chest bump with Brick Shithouse. Merlin hands Thomas a beer. Vicky pours Morgaine a glass of iced cold Sprite and asks when her baby is due (one month).

"Okay, get ready," I flag down our server and hand him my phone, "Group photo time!"

The server gestures for us to squeeze together. "Everybody raise your glasses. On the count of three. One..."

The Merlins peck me on the cheek.

Vicky smooths down her sleek career woman bob.

"Two..."

Mordred drapes his arms around his friends. Thomas clinks glasses with Brick Shithouse.

And Morgaine, seated next to me, takes my hand and squeezes it. I smile back at her. She's as stoic as ever, but her smoky eyes crinkle at the corners. I don't expect us to be BFFs, but I'm over the moon we're no longer mortal enemies.

"Three..."

*Snap.*

"Cheeeeeeeers!"

"Wait!" I check out the photo and hand my phone back to the server. "Let's take another and if you're able, maybe, kneel down on the ground so we can look taller?"

The entire table glares at me.

*"What?"*

——————

THANK you so much for reading my quirky little book. I hope it provided you with an escape and a few chuckles. If you had as much fun reading it as I had writing it, **please leave a review** on Amazon or your preferred book retailer.

Reviews help readers discover my books, motivating me to write *more* books. I read and learn from every review. Not only do your words help me improve, but I save screenshots from some of them to refer back to when I'm in my creative low. So you see, Dear Reader, your thoughts mean more than you know. Please leave a review:)


SIGN **up for my** NEWSLETTER to stay up to date on new releases and get a **free book** delivered to your inbox. An email from me is like a letter from a pen pal minus the postage. I aim to entertain you... infrequently but with a lot of passion.

# ABOUT THE AUTHOR

Teresa Yea is an awkward bean with a fondness for British period dramas and minimalism. In the grand scheme of romance novels, she likes dukes and viscounts, adorkable rom coms and spicy ebooks that blazes up her Kindle (you know the kind). She is obsessed with The Witch of Blackbird Pond, a book she has read over 15+ times and wrote about (lustfully) at her website tere sayea.com

She seriously wants you to SIGN UP for her NEWSLETTER (https://teresayea.com/newsletter/) where she aims to entertain you... infrequently but with a lot of passion.

Follow her on Instagram @teresayea. She has never influenced anyone, unless you count book recs.

Follow her on Facebook @teresayeawriter for romance novel swooning and Benedict Cumberbatch ogling.

She also penned some broody fantasies about Victorian monster hunters and that gothic one about a cursed ruby. All have sexy times, spice level: Sriracha.

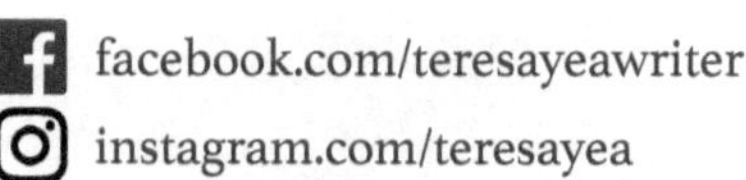

# ALSO BY TERESA YEA

Time Travelers (Chick Lit)
An Influencer in King Arthur's Court (#1)
Regency Influencer (#2)
Influencers Just Wanna Have Fun (#3)

Indigo Bay Series (Romantic Comedy)
Pixely Ever After (#1)
Once Upon a Photo Booth (#2)
Symphony in the Snow (#3)
Tea for Two (#4)

Bookish Romantics (Romantic Comedy)
Awkward in October (#1)
The Plant Nanny (#2)

Golden Age of Monsters (Dark Fantasy Romance)
Love in a Time of Monsters (#1)
Empire of Sand (prequel)

Gothic Horror
Black Heart, Red Ruby (standalone)